"I should have called. I'm sorry."

"It's all right, Dan." One corner of Bailey's mouth tipped up in a smile. "At least you came back this time."

He drew in a slow breath. "I did. But I've brought along a good many responsibilities that I didn't have when we talked before."

Bailey's gaze drifted back to the slumbering baby in her arms. "You sure have. And they're beautiful, Dan. Just beautiful."

True, but the twins were only part of what he'd been talking about—and honestly, not the part that worried him, at least not where Bailey was concerned. He'd known Bailey wouldn't blink about taking on a pair of orphaned twins. She was that kind of woman—the best kind, strong and sure and good.

"Everything's different now except for one thing. I still care about you, Bailey. I still want to see if we can work things out." He paused. "You say you were going to sign these papers because you thought that's what I wanted. It isn't, not by a long shot. But the question is, what do you want?"

Laurel Blount lives on a small farm in Middle Georgia with her husband, David, their four children, a milk cow, dairy goats, assorted chickens, an enormous dog, three spoiled cats and one extremely bossy goose with boundary issues. She divides her time between farm chores, homeschooling and writing, and she's happiest with a cup of steaming tea at her elbow and a good book in her hand.

Books by Laurel Blount

Love Inspired

A Rancher to Trust

Laurel Blount

HARLEQUIN® LOVE INSPIRED®

Recycling programs
for this product may
not exist in your area.

LOVE INSPIRED BOOKS

ISBN-13: 978-1-335-48792-6

A Rancher to Trust

www.Harlequin.com

Printed in U.S.A.

Therefore if any man be in Christ,
he is a new creature: old things are passed away;
behold, all things are become new.
—*2 Corinthians* 5:17

For Leigh M. Hall, my wild and crazy sister—
and my first and truest friend.

Chapter One

As Dan Whitlock pulled his pickup to a stop in the middle of the quiet Oklahoma cemetery, his cell phone buzzed against his chest for the third time. He fished it out of his shirt pocket and checked the screen. Sure enough, he had two missed calls and a text from rancher Colton McAllister.

Call me.

Dan looked out the truck window at the snowy cemetery and weighed his options. He'd planned to get this private errand over and done with before he touched base with Colt, but the new boss of the Bar M Ranch wasn't known for his patience. Might as well go ahead and call him back. Then maybe Dan could tend to his personal business in peace.

Colt answered the phone on the first ring. "About time."

"I was driving. Sorry, Colt, but my advice is pass on these heifers. They look a lot better on paper than they do in person. I know how bad you want to get in on the Shadow Lady bloodline, but trust me, these aren't your girls."

Colt made an irritated noise. "I should have figured as much. Price was too good. I'll start looking in a higher dollar range and see what I can find."

The Bar M didn't have that kind of money to play around with right now. Dan started to argue but thought better of it.

Not my call, he reminded himself, *not anymore*. As the elderly Gordon McAllister's foreman, Dan had overseen the day-to-day ranch operations. But now that Colt's grandfather had passed on, Colt had shifted from being Dan's friend to being Dan's boss. The younger McAllister preferred to handle things on his own.

"Anyway," Colt said, "I appreciate you taking a look. You about ready to head home?"

Dan's gaze drifted back to the scattered gravestones, sparkling icily in the brittle January sunlight. "Yeah, shortly. I have something I need to do first."

"No rush on this end. Take your time."

Dan could barely hear his friend's muffled words over the whistle of the Wyoming wind and the sound of cattle lowing. Colt probably had his phone clenched between his chin and his shoulder, which meant his hands were busy with something else.

"You out choring? I thought you were supposed to be helping Angie take care of those new twins of yours."

"I'm fixing that section of fence in the south pasture. I was going stir-crazy in the house, so Angie finally shooed me outside. Oh yeah. She said you had a phone call yesterday."

"Who from?"

"Some girl, Angie said. She wanted to talk to you,

wouldn't say why. Angie thought it might be something important, though, because the number came up Pine Valley, Georgia. Isn't that your hometown?"

Dan tightened his grip on the phone. "This girl. She give Angie a name?"

"Yeah. Bailey somebody, I think it was."

Bailey. Dan's skin prickled in a way that had nothing to do with the sharp air finding its way into the truck cab. "Bailey Quinn?"

"That sounds right." Something in his tone must have alerted Colt, because his friend added, "You sound like you just took a punch in the gut. Who's this Bailey girl to you?"

Dan didn't answer. He stared through the fogged windshield at a nearby tombstone, darkened with age, the name barely visible.

Who was Bailey to him?

At one point in his life—everything.

Now? She was a memory so full of regret that the pain could reach across more than a decade of time and stop his heart cold. And she definitely wasn't somebody he wanted to talk about. Not with Colt.

Not with anyone.

After a second or two of silence, Colt went on, "Angie told her you weren't here, and she left a number. Said she needed to talk to you, please, as soon as possible. Nice-sounding girl, Angie said."

"Text me the number." He tried not to ask, but he couldn't help it. "Did Bailey say anything else?"

"Not that Angie mentioned. Is this girl one of your folks, Dan? Because if you want to go back to Georgia and see about her, you go ahead. You're not needed here, so there's no reason for you to hurry back."

"Well, that's never a good thing to hear from an employer."

Colt made a frustrated noise. "You know what I mean. And you also know I don't think of you as an employee. You're family to me and Angie, just like you were to Grandpa. Maybe your last name isn't McAllister, but you're one of us, just the same."

You're one of us. High praise from one of the most clannish families in all of Wyoming. "You going mushy on me, Colt?"

"If I am, it's not my fault. It's the twins. Nobody's sleeping around here, and there's way too much crying."

"They're cute little stinkers, though." That was an understatement. Dan's honorary niece and nephew were so adorable they could make any man hungry to have a couple kids of his own.

"Yeah, they're cute, all right. That's how they suck you in. Trust me, Dan. This parenting-twins stuff is harder than ranching any day. No wonder I'm going soft. It's enough to send any man around the bend. I'll get Angie to text you that number. And listen, if you've got some kind of trouble brewing back home, you head there without a second thought, okay? We can manage until you get back."

"Thanks, Colt." Dan disconnected the phone and shoved it back into his pocket. He sat in the chilling truck cab, thinking hard.

So after all these years, Bailey Quinn had called him.

Her face came into his mind as clearly as if he'd seen her yesterday. Eyes such a rich, dark shade of brown that you could only make out her pupils if you were close enough to kiss her. He recalled the soft curve of her cheek and the sassy way she'd tilt her head when she was teasing you—which, Bailey being Bailey, was most of the time.

Years back, not long after hiring on at the Bar M, Dan had been out checking a fence line on a June morning. A pretty, dark-feathered bird perched on a strand of barbed wire had cocked its head at him in just the same way. Pain had ricocheted out of no-where with such force that his knees had almost buckled under him.

And that was just a dumb bird.

Even though the phone hadn't vibrated, he took it back out of his pocket and squinted at the screen. Nothing. Likely it would take Angie McAllister a while to get around to texting him Bailey's number. Colt's wife had her hands full wrangling their three-week-old babies, Josie and Finn.

In the meantime, Dan might as well do what he'd come here to do.

He turned the sound up on his phone so he wouldn't miss the text, got out of the truck and threaded his way through the graveyard, his boots crunching in the snow. It didn't take him long to find what he was looking for.

"Hey, there, Gordon." Dan removed his brown Stetson and then reached down and brushed the mounded snow from the top of his old boss's tombstone.

Gordon Finnley McAllister. The name was engraved deeply into solid gray granite Colt had chosen for his grandfather's memorial stone. It was one of the few decisions the new rancher had made that Dan hadn't privately second-guessed. Granite was a good fit for the stubborn old man he'd known.

Gordon McAllister's mind and body had been toughened by the wild land he loved, but the old rancher's

heart had been shaped by the Lord he'd followed faithfully—and gentled by the wife who lay slumbering
beside him now. Josephine Andrews McAllister had always missed her Oklahoma home, so Gordon had buried
her here, among her people. And when his time came,
he'd asked to be laid beside her instead of in his beloved
Wyoming. That request had shocked a lot of people back
in Broken Bow, given how passionately the old man had
loved the family ranch.

It hadn't shocked Dan at all. He knew Gordon had
loved his Josephine more.

Dan cleared his throat. "Colt wanted me to take a
look at some heifers a couple towns over, so I thought…
while I was in the neighborhood." This felt awkward.
But he forced himself to keep on going. "Colt's doing
you proud, Gordon. He's got the makings of a solid
rancher. Not as good as you, not yet. But one day he
will be. I've stayed on to help get him started, like I
promised you I would. But he's just about got his feet
under him now, and I'm thinking…" Dan fought the
lump that had risen up in his throat. This was hard.
"I'm thinking maybe it's getting time for me to up
stakes and move along. That's why I came by. To let
you know. And to bring you something."

He fished a brass token from his coat pocket. It
gleamed dully in the palm of his hand. "This is the
chip I got from my support group when I was one year
sober. You came to see me get it, eleven years ago this
March. Getting through that first year without a drink
was the first thing I'd done right in a long time, and one
of the toughest. I'd never have managed it without you
and that church you kept dragging me to. I've carried
this thing with me ever since, but now I'm leaving it

here with you." Dan gently placed the token on top of the grave marker. "I came here to thank you, Gordon McAllister, for taking me in and forgiving me when I didn't deserve it. I'll owe you a debt for the rest of my life, and me leaving the Bar M won't change that any. If Colt or Angie or those great-grandkids of yours ever need my help, I'll be there for them. No matter what. You've got my word on that."

He stood there for a long moment, his hand covering the token, the cold of the stone seeping into his fingers. Finally he lifted his hand and cleared his throat.

"That's all I needed to say, I guess. I'd best be getting along. Rest good, Gordon, here with your Josephine. You've earned it."

Then Dan settled his Stetson back on his head and started back toward the truck.

His phone chirped loudly just as he was settling into the seat. Angie had sent him a number, followed by, Colt says you go on to Georgia if you need to. Don't worry about us.

He wasn't worried about the McAllisters. Colt could run the Bar M just fine without Dan's help, even with a pair of brand-new babies thrown into the bargain.

But Dan had never planned to go back to Pine Valley, Georgia. He had his reasons for that, reasons that still tore him up when he allowed himself to think about them.

Which was why he didn't allow it.

Then again, if Bailey Quinn had reached out to him after what he'd done, after all these years…she must need something.

Something big.

He recalled something Gordon used to say when

they'd hit a snag in their work. "Sometimes you gotta go back a few fence posts, son, and fix a crooked one before you can go forward. Ain't no fun, but it's the right thing to do. Every man makes his share of mistakes, but they ain't nothing to be ashamed of unless you leave 'em standing."

Dan had left some pretty busted-up fence posts standing back in Pine Valley. He should have done what he could to fix them a long time ago, but he'd kept putting it off. It was no easy thing, going back to the place where you'd behaved the worst, facing up to what you'd done before you found your feet and your faith.

He was at a turning point right now. He was about to strike out on his own again, away from the shelter of the Bar M and the McAllisters. He needed all his fence posts as straight as he could get them, and it looked like God had just handed Dan an opportunity to get that done.

Whether he liked it or not.

Lord, what do You want me to do here?

Dan knew the answer almost before he'd finished the question. The things he'd done and the people he'd hurt—like Bailey Quinn—deserved a lot more from him than a phone call. It was long past time for him to face up to them and make whatever amends he could.

Dan looked back down at his phone and slowly typed out a reply.

Headed to Georgia. Tell Colt to text me if he needs anything.

Then he hit Send, dropped the phone on the seat and shoved the truck into first gear.

* * *

"Lucy Ball, drop that right now!" Bailey Quinn jogged around the corner of her old clapboard farmhouse, trying to keep the mischievous Jersey calf in sight. "You'll choke!"

The long-legged red calf tossed her head and flexed her jaw, crackling the plastic of the stolen water bottle she held clenched in her teeth. She was having fun, and she was in no hurry for this game to be over.

The calf loped by the chicken coop, making the young Barred Rock pullets flutter and cluck, before slowing to a stop by the open barn door. Bailey halted, too, just at the corner of the back porch, her heart pounding.

"That's right," she murmured coaxingly. "Go in there, where I might have a shot at cornering you!"

The valuable calf had been a farm-warming present from her friends Abel and Emily Whitlock.

Abel had shaken his head ruefully when Bailey thanked him. "Let's see how you feel in a year or so. I know you've been wanting a milk cow, but they're a sight more work than most people realize. They've got to be milked rain or shine, whether you're sick or not, Christmas Day same as any other. Then there's the milk you'll have to deal with. A good milker will give you gallons a day. That's a lot for one person to deal with. And you can't sell raw milk at that store of yours, not unless you get state certified, and that's near about more trouble and expense than it's worth."

Bailey had only laughed. She didn't care if owning a milk cow was going to be a lot of work. In fact, she was counting on it.

Now that her organic grocery store was well established, she'd been hungry for a new challenge. She missed the invigorating struggle of building up a fledgling business. Working hard was what made her feel alive. And the tougher the work, the more Bailey liked it.

Given how this was going, that was a good thing. The minute she'd seen the calf's fluffy red topknot, Bailey had christened her Lucille Ball after the iconic redheaded television star, and Lucy seemed determined to live up to her name. A day didn't go by that the animal didn't find some kind of trouble to get into. She was cute as could be, but right now Bailey almost wished Emily and Abel had given her a toaster.

Lucy blinked her long-lashed brown eyes at the barn doorway for a second or two. She gave her head another sassy shake, making the water slosh noisily inside the bottle. Then to Bailey's dismay, the calf kicked her heels and started off again, heading back toward the front yard.

Bailey blew out a sigh. "I do not have time for this today," she informed her squawking chickens as she stalked past them.

She really didn't, but she fought a smile as she spoke. Yes, she had a lot to do, but she wasn't complaining. This crazy overload was exactly the tonic she'd needed.

It wasn't just the store. She'd been feeling restless for about a year now, ever since bookstore owner Anna Delaney had married Hoyt Bradley. Since then, Anna and Hoyt had welcomed their first baby together. Another friend, pastor's wife Natalie Stone, was expecting her second child in a few months. And Emily Whitlock had not one but two sets of twins to take care of, in addition to managing the local coffee shop.

Bailey was over-the-moon happy for them all, but lately she'd felt her usual zest for life ebbing a bit. Okay. A lot. It was just that, compared to all the exciting and meaningful stuff going on with her friends, Bailey's life had seemed a little…

Boring.

Well, not anymore. Not since she'd gone to that informational meeting about foster parenting hosted by Anna's bookstore, Turn the Page.

Bailey had only gone to help Anna with the refreshments and to support Jillian Marshall, the local social worker who was giving the presentation. Bailey had never expected to walk out of there with a packet of paperwork clutched in her hand and a new dream burning in her heart.

But she had. The pictures of those little faces had stirred up a dream she'd given up on a long time ago. As the "surprise" only child of older parents, Bailey had longed for brothers and sisters. She'd promised herself that someday she'd raise a big, rambunctious family of her own—preferably on a farm with plenty of animals and homegrown vegetables.

At the time, of course, she'd assumed she'd share that life with…somebody special.

That part hadn't worked out the way she'd hoped. But according to Jillian, single women could be foster moms. That nugget of information was a game changer. Bailey could build her dream family all by herself by giving a loving home to kids who needed one.

And since she couldn't do that in a cramped apartment, Bailey's first order of business had been sinking all her savings into a down payment on the biggest house with the largest acreage she could afford. Which also happened to be a really old house that needed an awful lot of work.

Jillian had shaken her head when Bailey had given her a tour. "Honey, I hate to tell you, but this place is going to have to be overhauled from top to bottom if you want to pass the home-study safety inspection."

Bailey hadn't flinched, even though her bank account was anemic now. "No problem. Just tell me what I need to do, and I'll find a way to do it."

"Well, for starters, you're going to have to put a fence around that pond there. Bodies of water have to be fenced off. It's a rule."

When Abel had heard about that, he'd trucked over some extra fencing material he'd had on hand. Bailey had argued, but all she'd gotten was a lecture on looking gift horses in their mouths.

So fencing was today's project. Unfortunately, it wasn't going well, even without the impromptu calf chases. So far, she'd gotten exactly three fence posts in, and she'd been at it for an hour and a half. She definitely had her work cut out for her.

But first she had to catch that ridiculous calf. The question was, how?

As she walked by the barn, an idea struck her. She ducked inside and scooped a small amount of grain into a bucket.

When she rounded the side of the house, she saw Lucy standing in the front yard, nosing the water bottle along the ground. When the calf heard Bailey approaching, the animal picked up her stolen toy and tensed, ready to scamper off again.

"See what I have?" Bailey rattled the bucket.

The calf took three curious steps in her direction and halted. Bailey shook the grain again. That did it. Lucy dropped the bottle and trotted in Bailey's direction. Bailey backed up slowly, leading the calf toward the barn and jiggling her bucket enticingly with every step.

Five minutes later, Bailey was latching the big wooden doors behind her and dusting off her hands.

One problem solved, fifty bazillion to go. And she had no idea how she was going to manage most of them.

But, she reminded herself, Jacob Stone's last sermon had been all about how God often called ill-equipped people to do His work. "If you feel like what you're being called to do is impossible but is something the world needs, you're probably on the right track," the minister had said. "Just focus on doing what you can and trust Him for the rest of it. And always be prepared for Him to work things out differently than you might expect."

Well, Bailey couldn't wait to see what God was going to do with her situation, and if He wanted to tuck some surprises in along the way, that was fine by her. After a year of feeling purposeless and bored, this excitement was a welcome change.

On her way across the yard, she stooped and picked up Lucy's discarded plastic bottle. Returning to her fence, she stashed the slobbery container next to the last post she'd managed to get in and pulled on her work gloves. She hefted up her new post-hole diggers and focused on the spot she'd marked for the next post. Raising the heavy diggers as high as she could, she rammed them downward, biting into the soft brown soil.

She'd clamped out three more skimpy scoops of dirt when she heard the sound of a vehicle crunching up her rutted driveway. She turned to see a silver Ford pickup nosing its way toward her.

Just what she didn't need right now. Company. Oh well. Maybe it was a friend she could draft into helping her get this fence up while they visited.

Bailey's eyes narrowed as she got a better look at the truck. She knew pretty much everybody's vehicle around here, but she didn't recognize this one. It was a newer model, but it had the dings and scrapes of a work truck. She squinted, but the afternoon sun was glaring off the windshield. All she could tell about the driver was that he was wearing a cowboy hat.

Definitely not from around here, then.

Curious now, she studied the approaching vehicle, stripping off her canvas gloves and dropping them on the ground. Who could this cowboy be, and what was he doing way out here?

Only one way to find out. The truck rolled to a stop, and Bailey headed toward it. The driver unfolded himself from the cab when she was about half the way across the yard. He was tall and lean, but there was a muscular set to his shoulders. Too bad she *didn't* know him. This guy could probably set a fence post in no time.

"Hey, there," she called in a friendly voice. "You lost?"

The man had been scanning her place, but he turned his head toward her when she spoke. When he did, more than fifteen years of Bailey's life crumbled away, leaving her face-to-face with a part of her past she'd tried very hard to forget.

Dan Whitlock.

Bailey stumbled to a halt, not quite believing her eyes. But it was true. After all these years, Dan was standing in her driveway.

For the past couple of days, ever since she'd dialed the Wyoming number she'd found on the internet, Bailey had been jumping every time her phone rang. She'd wondered if Dan would even call her back—and how she'd handle it if he did.

But he hadn't called her back. He'd shown up in person.

She had absolutely no idea what to do right now.

He touched the brim of his hat. "Ma'am." The voice was definitely Dan's, but the gentle drawl of the deep South had been melded with something else, something stronger and brisker. "I'm sorry to trouble you, but a fellow back in town told me I might find a girl named Bailey Quinn up this way. Would you happen to know where she lives?"

Bailey had to swallow twice before she could speak. "It's me," she managed finally. "Dan, it's me."

"Bailey?" As Dan moved toward her, she saw that his voice wasn't the only thing that had changed. He walked with the rolling gait of a man accustomed to spending a good portion of his day on horseback, and he limped a little on his left leg.

As he came close, he pulled the hat off his head. Not everything about him had changed. His hair was still the same dark mahogany, its waves pressed flat against his head. The same greenish-brown eyes skimmed over her, head to toe, before meeting her own.

He looked every bit as dumbfounded as she felt.

"It *is* you! Man, I'm sorry. I didn't recognize you at first. You look so…different." His eyes dropped to the teeth that had endured five long years of belated braces to correct her overbite.

Now that he was standing right in front of her, the memories Dan had jarred loose felt even more over-whelming. Her heart was thudding so hard it actually hurt.

Bailey took a deep breath. *Settle down*, she told herself firmly. *You can handle this.*

She could. She didn't just look different. She *was* different. The night Dan had left her had marked the lowest point in her life. But after a few weeks of wallowing in self-pity, she'd washed her tear-splotched face and decided enough was enough.

Over the next few months, she'd toned up, given up sugar, ditched her glasses for contacts and straightened her crooked teeth. And while everybody else raved over how different she looked, Bailey knew the really important changes had happened on the inside.

She stood on her own two feet now, and she trusted her head a lot more than she trusted her heart. She'd learned those lessons the hard way, and she couldn't afford to forget them, no matter who pulled up in her driveway.

She forced a shrug. "It's been a long time, Dan. People change."

"Yeah." He nodded slowly. "I guess they do."

An awkward silence fell between them. Finally, Bailey raised an eyebrow. "Well, now that the pleasantries are out of the way, I guess we can move on to the main event. Why are you here, Dan?"

"You called me."

"I called you," Bailey repeated. He made it sound so simple, as if the two of them facing each other after all this time wasn't the most complicated thing that had ever happened in her entire life. Her jangled nerves found that ridiculously funny. She tried her best to swallow her laugh, but it just came out through her nose in a strangled snort. "And instead of—I don't know—calling me back, you decided to drive all the way here from Wyoming?"

"I wasn't in Wyoming. I was in Oklahoma tending to some business. Not that it would have mattered." He drew in a long breath. "I'd have driven here from Alaska, if that's where I'd been. You and I both know that I owe you that much. At least."

"Maybe you do." Bailey saw no point in skirting the truth. "But I gave up on collecting that debt a long time ago."

He didn't flinch. "I figured. That's how I knew this had to be about something important. You'd never have called me otherwise. It's true, what you said a minute ago. People do change. I've changed. I don't expect you to take my word on that, but it's why I'm here. So just tell me what you need from me. If there's any way I can give it to you, it's yours. No questions asked."

Bailey's knees had started wobbling, and that irritated her. The unfairness of this whole situation irritated her. She wasn't supposed to be standing two feet away from Dan while they had this conversation. All of this was supposed to happen over the phone, and that would have been plenty tough enough, thank you very much.

She wasn't prepared for this.

But she should have been. She, of all people, should have known that Dan Whitlock had a knack for sending a person's well-crafted plans spinning sideways.

She clamped her hands together, digging her short fingernails into her palms. "I'm glad to hear you say that, Dan. Because the truth is, you're right. There *is* something I need from you."

"Okay." His eyes never left hers. "Name it."

"A divorce."

Chapter Two

He couldn't have heard that right. "A *what*?"

"A divorce," Bailey repeated.

"But we're not still…" He stalled out, searching her face. "I mean, didn't you…?" He watched as a flush heated Bailey's cheeks. "Bailey, are you telling me we're still *married*?"

"Yes." There was a little muscle twitching in her cheek, but she held her ground. "I don't know why you're acting so surprised. You were there."

"But that was years ago." He stopped and shook his head. "I figured you'd have dealt with it, had it annulled or whatever people do. In fact, I was pretty sure that was the first thing you'd have done after I…left."

The flush in Bailey's cheeks deepened. "Better late than never."

Dan searched his mind for something to say, but he came up with nothing. "Maybe I was a little quick on the trigger with that no-questions-asked thing. Is there someplace we could sit down while we talk this over?"

Bailey hesitated then nodded reluctantly. "We can sit on the porch if you want, but there's really not much to talk about. The whole thing should be very straight-forward."

Straightforward wasn't the word Dan would have picked. He'd been trampled by bulls and walked away feeling more clearheaded than he felt right now.

All these years, he'd been *married* to Bailey Quinn? It was more than he could take in. The feelings he'd kept corralled in the deepest part of his heart were stampeding in fifty different directions. The dust was going to have to settle some before he could make sense of all of this.

He hadn't even wrapped his mind around the fact that the woman standing in front of him was really Bailey. She looked so different from the girl he remembered.

Back in high school she'd carried a few extra pounds that softened her figure, and her front teeth had been a little crooked. She'd always worn a pair of dark-rimmed glasses that had slid to the end of her nose about every five minutes. She was forever pushing them back up with an impatient finger, and he was forever plucking them off so that he could steal a kiss.

All those things had just made Bailey cuter.

He could think of a lot of words to describe Bailey now, but *cute* wasn't one of them. This new Bailey was lean and fit, with perfectly straight teeth and a don't-mess-with-me way of looking straight at you.

She was beautiful, sure. No man alive would dispute that. But it was a whole different kind of beauty than he remembered.

Now this woman he barely recognized was telling him she was his *wife*?

The man he'd spoken to back in town had told him

Bailey had just bought this place. The closer Dan and Bailey got to the farmhouse, the more he wondered why. Bailey had her work cut out for her, all right. The house had good bones, but it needed lot of repairs.

There were no chairs on the porch, so he settled carefully on the splintered steps. After an awkward pause, Bailey joined him. She positioned herself against the sagging wooden handrail, leaving a generous space between them. The shadow of the overhanging roof blocked the thin warmth of the January sun, but the sudden chill Dan felt had little to do with the weather.

In the old days Bailey would have cuddled close to him, settling her head in the gap between his shoulder and his neck. He could still remember exactly how that had made him feel at nineteen. Fiercely protective and defiantly happy, at a time in his life when happiness had been pretty hard to come by.

Now the very same girl was treating him like a stranger. He'd earned the coolness in those beautiful brown eyes, every bit of it.

But, man, oh man. The pain of seeing it there was almost more than he could stand.

Dan cleared his throat. "Okay. First off, how is this even possible?"

Bailey cocked her eyebrows. "We eloped, Dan. To Tennessee, remember?"

Yeah, he remembered. He'd just gotten dinged by the county sheriff for underage drinking again, and Bailey's long-suffering parents had handed down an ultimatum. If he wanted to attend church with them, fine. That much they'd allow, although they didn't sound too enthusiastic about the idea. But they made it clear that their daughter wasn't to spend any more time alone with him. He wouldn't be allowed to drive Bailey anywhere or take her out to dinner. It was plain enough that Mr. and Mrs. Quinn were more than ready to put a stop to a relationship they'd never really approved of in the first place.

The idea of being separated from Bailey had sent Dan into a tailspin. She was the one good thing in his out-of-control life, the only person in the whole town who hadn't heard his last name and shied away from him. But her parents, along with everybody else in Pine Valley, seemed sure that he and Abel would turn out to be drunks and thieves, just like their dad and uncles had been, and their granddad before that.

And deep down, he'd been scared that—in his case, anyway—they were dead right. At nineteen, his drinking was already starting to get away from him, and he'd tangled with the law a few times. Nothing big, not yet. But without Bailey in his life…well, he'd known exactly what that would mean for him.

He'd self-destruct fast.

The fear had made him desperate and angry—and selfish. So selfish that one moonlit June night, he'd sweet-talked the eighteen-year-old girl he loved into leaving her parents' tidy brick home and running away with him.

He'd never forgive himself for that.

Bailey was still waiting for his answer. He swallowed. "I know we *were* married. But we haven't laid eyes on each other in years."

Bailey gave a frustrated laugh. "A marriage certificate doesn't have an expiration date, Dan. It's not a jug of milk."

"Well, no. But after I…" He stopped short.

"Ran off and left me at that awful motel in Kentucky?" Bailey's eyes hardened as she finished his sentence. "You thought that made the marriage evaporate? Well, it didn't."

He winced. "You've got every right to be mad, Bailey. I deserve that for talking you into the whole elopement idea and then leaving you to clean up the mess all by yourself. I knew you'd have to do things. Fill out papers and all that. I'd always assumed that's what you did."

"Trust me, I wish I had taken care of it back then, but I didn't. So we have to deal with it now. Let's stay focused on that."

"Hold on a minute." He studied Bailey. That muscle was jumping in her cheek again, and there was a tenseness about her body that he recognized with the instinct of a man who'd spent most of his last decade moving cattle. She wanted to bolt. Something about this conversation was spooking her.

"Dan—" she started off again, but he interrupted, intent on circling back to the territory that was puzzling him.

"I'm sorry. I sure don't have any right to question how you handled things, but this just isn't making any sense to me. Your parents couldn't even stand the idea of me being your boyfriend. Me being your husband? That must have sent them straight into orbit. Mind you, looking back I can't say as I blame them. How come they didn't take you to file the paperwork five minutes after you got back home?" He couldn't think of a single reason they wouldn't have.

Bailey sighed, but she met his eyes squarely. "Because I never told them we got married."

Okay. Except for that.

"You didn't...what do you mean you never told them?"

"I didn't tell anybody." She looked away and continued in a rush, "Look, none of that really matters now, does it? We were young, and we made a mistake. I didn't call you to rehash the past. I called you because I'm ready to move on with my life, and there are certain things I can't do until we get this settled."

Certain things. The confused feelings swooping around in Dan's chest turned to stone and dropped heavily into the pit of his stomach.

So that's what this was about. Bailey had fallen in love with another guy—probably wanted to get married. But she couldn't, not while she was still legally bound to Dan.

When Dan didn't respond, Bailey glanced at him. His expression had changed. The sun creases in the corners of his eyes had deepened, and his jaw was set. He looked tired.

And a little sad.

He caught her eye. "I get what you're saying about leaving the past behind. No man who's made the kind of mistakes I've made would argue with you. But before we do, I'd like to give you an overdue apology. If you'll let me."

He was holding his hat in his hands, running the brim slowly around in a circle. He watched her face, waiting to see if she was willing to hear him out.

She wasn't. She was holding herself together by a

thread, and this wasn't a road she wanted to go down right now.

"You don't need to apologize, Dan. I'll admit it hurt when you walked out on me, but in time I realized that even if you'd come back that night, things couldn't have worked out any differently in the long run. We never should have gotten married in the first place."

"And that's completely on me. I never should have talked you into it. But, Bailey, back then I was so in love with you. I was scared to death I was going to lose you, and—"

"Please. Just stop." Bailey stood. She'd had just about all she could take. "This isn't all on you, Dan. It's not like you kidnapped me. I *let* you talk me into eloping. And honestly, I was such a pushover, you could've talked me into just about anything. The way I see it, I'm just as much to blame as you are, and I take full responsibility for my own mistake. Now, I appreciate you driving all this way, but it really wasn't necessary. Once the divorce papers are drawn up, I'll just need your notarized signature, and it'll be a done deal."

"All right." He had stayed seated and was looking up at her, his expression carefully blank. "I'll make sure you get it."

"Thanks." Bailey reached into her shirt pocket and pulled out a crumpled scrap of paper and a pen. "Write down your email address, and I'll be in touch. Now, if you'll excuse me, I really need to get back to work." She hesitated awkwardly, unsure what she should say or do next. How exactly did you end a conversation like this with some kind of dignity? She had no idea.

Finally, she reached out a hand and laid it gently

on his bicep. It felt like touching a sun-warmed rock. "Goodbye, Dan."

She turned away and headed across the yard to the unfinished fence. Leaning over, she snagged the work gloves she'd dropped on the ground...what? Twenty minutes ago, maybe?

It felt like a lifetime.

Her hands were shaking so much that she had a hard time getting her fingers into the right slots. When the gloves were finally on, she reached for the post-hole diggers. As she jammed them back into the hole she'd begun, she heard the boards of the porch steps creak.

Okay, good. Dan was leaving. She held her breath, waiting to hear his truck door open and close.

"Bailey." He spoke from so close behind her that she jumped like a startled deer. "Sorry. I didn't mean to spook you. But...what you said back there. You were wrong. I did come back."

She flashed him an irritated glance. "What are you talking about?"

"I drove around for a few hours. Did some drinking." His fingers were clenched down so hard on the weathered brim of his hat that his knuckles were white. "But then I came back to the motel room. It was about three thirty in the morning, and you were curled up asleep on the bed with wadded-up tissues all around you. You'd been crying—hard—and you almost never cried. I'd done that to you on our wedding day, because I'd fought with you about driving back to Pine Valley and facing up to your parents."

"Dan, like I said, there's no point in—"

He cut her off. "I told you I wanted to go west, start fresh someplace new, just the two of us. But the truth was, I was just a coward. I was scared if we went back to Georgia, your parents would talk you into getting out of the marriage. Why wouldn't they? I was a nineteen-year-old boy with a pretty serious drinking problem, a bad reputation and zero skills that would help me land a job. And standing there looking down at you, I knew they were right. I was going to ruin your life."

He stopped. When he spoke again, his voice was rough with conviction. "I don't think I ever sobered up as fast in my life as I did that night. And yeah, I left you there. It was the hardest thing I ever did. I'm really sorry I hurt you, but when I think about some of the things that happened to me after that, some of the places I ended up before I finally got myself turned around... Well, I can only thank the good Lord that I didn't hurt you even worse."

Bailey stared at him, the post-hole diggers still clenched in her hands. What was she supposed to say to that?

After a second or two, he cleared his throat. "About this divorce thing. Lawyers can get pricey. I'd like to cover the cost."

"I'm not asking you to do that."

"I know you're not. But I want to, just the same. How long will it take get it all settled?"

Bailey blinked and swallowed hard. "I don't know. I'll have to meet with the lawyer and see how soon he can draw up the papers. Did you leave me your email?"

"I wrote it down." He offered her the scrap of paper she'd left behind on the porch step. She took it, careful not to brush his fingers with hers, and tucked it back into the breast pocket of her shirt.

"Okay. I'll be in touch once I know more."

"Would it speed things up any if I stayed in Pine Valley until the papers are ready?"

Bailey bit her lip. He wanted to stick around town? The idea made her uneasy. "That's not necessary. Besides, you've probably got things you need to tend to back home."

"Nothing more important than this. I came here to do whatever I could to set things right, Bailey. I can stay for as long as you need me to."

"Like I said, all I need is your signature, and we can handle that long-distance." She hesitated, but in the end she couldn't resist adding, "But if you're serious about setting things straight around here, you should stop by and make your peace with your brother before you leave."

Dan flinched. "Abel still lives around here?"

"He does, but not at the old cabin. He lives on Goosefeather Farm with his wife and kids now. He married Emily Elliott a few years ago."

"Is that so? He always was crazy about Emily, but he never figured she'd look twice at him. And he's ended up with Mrs. Sadie's farm to boot. He loved that place." Dan's wary expression softened. "Isn't that something? Well, I'm glad it all worked out for him."

Bailey hesitated, but the sadness in Dan's eyes and her long-standing friendship with Abel overrode her reluctance to meddle. "You should stop and see them, Dan. It would mean the world to Abel."

Dan shook his head absently, his eyes lingering on the semicircle of pines crowding the edge of the sparkling pond. "I doubt that. But maybe I will. I came here to face up to the messes I left behind. If Abel wants to take a swing at me, it's no more than I deserve."

"I think Abel might surprise you. But if you don't mind, could you keep our situation quiet? I wasn't kidding before when I said I didn't tell anybody about our marriage. Abel doesn't know, either, and since it's all about to be over and done with anyway, I don't see much point in telling him about it now."

"I don't imagine I'll be on Abel's property long enough to do a whole lot of talking, so don't worry yourself. He won't hear about it from me."

Bailey nodded. "Thanks. If there's nothing else, I really do need to get this fence up."

"Need some help? Because I could—"

"No." She cut off the offer quickly. "I'll manage. But thanks."

"All right, then. I'll leave you be." He settled his cowboy hat back on his head. His eyes were instantly shadowed, but she could feel them on her face, studying her. "I'll be seeing you, I reckon."

Her heart jolted at the idea. "Like I said, I'll be in touch once I've heard back from the lawyer." She stuck out her gloved hand. "I know things are—different between us now. But I'm glad to see you're doing so well, Dan. I truly am."

He took her hand and held it gently for a second or two. Even through the roughness of the glove, she could feel the strong warmth of his fingers. "It's good seeing you, too, Bailey. Doing so well."

Flustered, she nodded. She pulled her hand free and turned back toward the fence line.

"Be careful." He spoke quietly behind her just as she jammed the diggers into the dirt. "Set those posts in good and straight. Take it from me, it's a lot of trouble trying to fix up the crooked ones later."

Once Dan's pickup had rumbled out of the drive-way, Bailey sucked in a long, deep breath and bent to rest her head on the wooden handles of the post-hole diggers. She stood that way for several long minutes until her heartbeat slowed back down to something closer to normal.

Then she straightened up, wiped her eyes briskly on her sleeve and went back to work.

Chapter Three

Later that afternoon Dan clenched his jaw as he turned into the long gravel driveway leading to Goosefeather Farm. It was taking every ounce of his willpower to keep the truck pointed toward his brother's new home.

This probably wasn't a good idea, going out to see Abel right now. Dan was reeling from his talk with Bailey. Just seeing her again would've been hard enough, but discovering he was still married to her?

He hadn't been ready for that—or for finding out she'd fallen for some other guy.

That part probably shouldn't have hit him as hard as it had, given the circumstances. But it had thrown him some, and maybe he should've taken some time to lick his wounds before signing up for a third punch in the gut.

Still, he'd come to Pine Valley to mend what fences he could—not that his plan was working out all that well. Bailey had been polite enough, but it was plain that all she wanted was to see the back of him. He couldn't blame her for that.

His brother would likely feel the same. On the posi-

tive side, no matter what Abel said or did, it couldn't
hurt him any worse than seeing Bailey had.

Dan reached the end of the winding driveway and
studied the view through his windshield. Goosefeather
Farm had prospered under Abel. The old white house
looked snug and well kept, flanked by rolling pastures,
green with a winter crop of rye grass. Even the big barn
sported a fresh coat of dark red paint.

Dan wasn't surprised. Abel had always done his best
to take good care of whatever ended up on his plate,
including his ornery younger brother. As a young teen-
ager, Dan hadn't much appreciated Abel's fumbling at-
tempts to fill their drunken father's shoes. In fact, he'd
fought Abel every inch of the way, and he'd followed
that up by leaving town without so much as a goodbye.

Dan sat for a minute as the winter sun beat through
his windshield. Abel had every reason to bear a grudge,
and most likely this wasn't going to go well. It didn't
matter. His brother was long overdue for this apology,
whether he was willing to accept it or not.

One thing was for sure. Dan had better get what
old Gordon used to call "prayed up" before getting out
of this truck. He bowed his head and closed his eyes.

*God, help me face up to my brother and tell him I'm
sorry for all the trouble I caused him. And no matter
what he says or how mad he gets, help me to remember that he's got every right to feel that way. Amen.*

When Dan lifted his head, he saw movement out
of the corner of his eye. Abel had stepped to the wide
doorway of the barn and was looking in Dan's direction.

Unlike Bailey, Abel hadn't changed much. He was
still lean and tall, a muscled scarecrow with a shock

of black hair. He was wiping his fingers on a greasy rag as he squinted at the truck. Dan wasn't surprised that he'd caught his brother working. Abel had never been one to sit idle.

Abel tossed up a hand in a friendly greeting and started across the yard. Dan felt sweat break out under the brim of his hat, but he switched the truck off and pushed open the door. Drawing in a deep breath of air that smelled richly of cows and hay, he walked around the front of the truck and faced his brother for the first time in over fifteen years.

"Hey, there!" The familiarity of his brother's deep voice hit Dan hard in the pit of his stomach. "Don't usually see Wyoming plates around here. What can I do for you?"

Dan cleared his throat. "Abel, it's—"

Those two words were as far as he got. Abel froze. Then he flung the greasy rag to the side, and before Dan realized what was happening, he was tackled in a hug that made his ribs howl in protest. Abel's voice spoke roughly in his ear.

"Danny, it's really you! You're finally home! Thank You, God! Thank You!"

Abel must have been working on a piece of farm machinery, because the odor of diesel fuel was coming off him in waves so strong that Dan's eyes watered.

Although it could be that the fumes weren't the only reason for that.

Dan swallowed the lump in his throat, put his arms awkwardly around his brother and hugged him back. "It's good to see you, too, Abel."

"*Good*'s not even close to being a big enough word for this." Abel pulled back to look him in the eye, but his older brother kept a firm grip on Dan's upper arms, as if he were afraid to let go. "I've been praying for this for so long, I'd just about given up on God ever answering me. But here you are!"

Dan had been braced for a chewing out, maybe even for a punch in the nose. He deserved both of them for running off like he had, for sending no word back for so long.

He hadn't expected this kind of welcome, and he didn't know what to say. Except...

"Abel, I'm so sorry. I shouldn't have—"

"Nope." Abel grabbed him again in another bear hug, this time knocking the Stetson clean off Dan's head. "I'm not listening to any apologies. You're home, and that's all that matters to me."

"Abel?" A feminine voice called from the direction of the house. "Is everything all right?"

Dan looked over Abel's shoulder. A slender woman with masses of light hair falling around her shoulders was standing on the steps of the farmhouse. Twin toddlers with Abel's black hair peeked shyly from behind her skirt.

"Better than all right, Emily!" Abel's voice shook as he answered his wife. "Danny's come home!"

"Oh, Abel! That's wonderful! Well, don't keep him all to yourself! Come on into the kitchen, Danny! I just took some fresh bread out of the oven." She beckoned enthusiastically and then turned, taking her children's hands and leading them back into the house.

"I don't want to butt in—" Dan ducked down to rescue his hat, and when he straightened up, Abel flung one arm around his younger brother's shoulders and began herding him toward the house.

"'Course you're coming in! I've got kids for you to meet, Uncle Danny! I want to hear all about what you've been doing since you left town." Abel led the way across a screened side porch and opened a door, ushering Dan inside.

The farmhouse kitchen closed around him with as much warmth as his brother's unexpected hug. The room was clean and bright, with red-checkered curtains and flowers blooming cheerfully on a sunny window-sill. Two golden-brown loaves of bread were cooling on the counter, and children's toys littered the floor.

Before Dan knew what was happening, he was settled in a chair at the big oval table. A thick slice of bread sat in front of him, homemade butter melting into golden streams across its top. Emily set a steaming cup of coffee at his elbow before turning to pour cups of milk for the twins.

The toddlers were staring at him owlishly. The boy had Abel's blue eyes, but the girl had inherited her mother's green ones.

Keeping one wary eye fixed on Dan, the little girl flickered pleading fingers at her father, who immediately gathered her gently onto his knees. The boy stood his ground, watching the stranger closely, one thumb stuck in his mouth.

"That's your uncle Danny," Abel told them. "Dan, this little sweetheart is our Lily, and the fine-looking fellow over there is Luke. They just turned two back in December."

"Hi." The kids were cute as they could be. What must it be like, Dan wondered, to have a wife you loved and a home like this? Nice, he reckoned. "You've got yourself a fine family, Abel."

"And this isn't all of it." Abel grinned up at his wife. "There's two more of us. Paul and Phoebe are visiting their nana Lois for the afternoon. I sure hate they're missing this, but I suppose you'll meet them soon enough."

"Four kids." Not only was Dan an uncle, he was an uncle four times over. It was a lot to take in, and he felt a twinge of envy. If things had been different, if he and Bailey had stayed together, maybe they'd have kids by now, too. "That's really something."

"Well, Phoebe and Paul came along with Emily when I married her, so I got a triple blessing there. You have any kids, Danny?"

"No. I'm not—" *Married.* That's what he'd started to say, but that wasn't true. "I'm not as blessed as you are," he finished awkwardly.

"Well now, don't give up hope. Sometimes God works things out slow, but He always gets the job done in His good time. The fact that you're sitting here at my table today is proof enough of that. I sure have a lot to thank Him for. You mind if I go ahead and get started on that now? We generally say grace before we eat, but if it bothers you—"

"Nope." As off balance as he felt right now, Dan's answer came fast and sure. "The Lord's seen me through some hard times, Abel. I wouldn't be sitting here in front of you it hadn't been for Him and the good people He set in my path. So you go right ahead."

Joy sparkled in Abel's eyes. "That's real good to hear, Danny. Come on, kids, let's pray."

Dan closed his eyes and listened to his brother's deep voice. "Lord, I thank You for bringing my brother home to me. And please forgive me for all those times

I got kinda short with You about how long it was taking. I should've known You were up to something bigger than I could think to ask You for. You've not only brought Danny back, You've brought him back knowing You. That's a double gift, and now I'm grateful You took Your time. I surely am."

Dan felt a little hand come to rest on top of his. Startled, he opened his eyes. Luke had edged closer, and he was gripping Dan's thumb in one chubby fist. The toddler had his eyes squeezed tightly shut, his face puckered in concentration.

Dan quickly followed suit, doing his best to refocus his attention on his brother's brief prayer.

"Amen," Abel finished, and Luke's eyes popped open.

"Amen," the little boy echoed cheerfully. He loosened his grasp on Dan's finger and then reached out to cautiously touch the Stetson Dan had placed on the table.

Dan grinned as he studied his nephew. Cowboy hats drew little boys as sure as flowers drew honeybees.

What would it be like to have a son like this little fellow? Somebody to teach and love and look after? He'd probably never know, and most likely that was a good thing. Abel was prime father material, no doubt about it. Dan not so much.

Still. It might have been kind of nice.

"Let's not get Uncle Danny's hat all sticky, Lukey," his mother said. Emily flashed an apologetic smile at Dan. "He had that thumb in some jam just a second ago."

"That's all right." Dan picked the hat up and settled it on his nephew's head. It swallowed the little boy, making his parents chuckle. Luke poked the brim up with one hand and grinned from under it with such cheeky joy that Dan's heart gave another strangely painful twist.

"Now then," Abel said, reaching for the mason jar of homemade strawberry jam his wife had placed on the table. He scooted it in Dan's direction. "Spread some of this on that bread there and let's get ourselves all caught up."

An hour later, there were only crumbs on the plates, and Emily had refilled Dan's coffee cup for the third time. Abel leaned back in his chair and shook his head.

"So my baby brother's a rancher now. The Bar M. I sure would like to see that place. I'm such a homebody, I've never been farther west than Alabama myself."

"I'd love to have you come out west for a visit, Abel, but the truth is, I may not be at the Bar M much longer."

"Why not? You don't get along with this new Colt fellow?"

Dan shook his head. "It's not that. Colt McAllister's a good man, and we've been friends for years. But he doesn't need the same kind of foreman his grandpa did. Mr. Gordon was in his seventies when I hired on, and he'd had two heart attacks. It's different with Colt. Colt's young and healthy, and he likes to handle things himself instead of relying on an employee. Nothing wrong with that. I'd be that way myself, probably."

Abel nodded. "But it's tough to step back when you've been the one running the show. Is that it?"

"Something like that, I reckon. Colt will put in a good word for me, and folks trust the McAllisters. I shouldn't have much trouble hiring on someplace else, once I put out the word that I'm looking." Dan darted an uneasy look at his brother's face. "It's not pride, Abel. I've always known my place. It's just—"

"You don't have to explain," Abel interrupted him. "I can see for myself how it is. You've grown too big for the space this Colt fellow can give you. That's all. You need to find yourself a place where you can flex your muscles a little. A place of your own, maybe." His brother's eyes lit up. "I'd sure be happy if you settled down somewhere close to Pine Valley."

"Not likely. I never fit here the way you do, Abel. You know that."

"Seems to me you've changed a good bit since you've been away, Danny. Could be you'd fit in here better than you think. But I reckon that's something you'll need to find out for yourself. Either way, you won't be leaving right away, I hope. You can stay on a few days, at least, can't you?"

Dan hesitated, but then he nodded. "Yeah, I guess I could." He owed Abel that much, and maybe by then the divorce papers would be ready to sign. Then he could put Pine Valley in his rearview mirror with a clear conscience.

"Good! You can bunk up at the old cabin. I use the workshop behind it for my wood-carving business, but other than that the place has been standing empty since Emily and I got married."

The cabin? Dan shook his head quickly. "I don't want to put you to any bother."

"It's no bother, and that cabin's as much yours as it is mine, Danny."

Maybe so, but Dan would just as soon never lay eyes on that place again. The memories associated with the cabin where he'd grown up weren't good ones. But that's what this whole visit was about, wasn't it? Facing up to the past he'd been running away from.

All of it. Whether he liked it or not.

"All right, if you're sure I won't be troubling you any. Thanks." Dan shot a wary glance at the staircase. Emily had disappeared up that way a few minutes ago with the twins in tow, saying she was going to settle them down for a nap. It was quiet up there now, so Emily might be coming back down soon.

If Dan was going to ask the question burning a hole in his gut, now would probably be the best time. "Hey, Abel? How's Bailey Quinn doing these days?"

"Bailey? She's doing all right. She'll be happy to hear you're back in town. After you left, she nearly pestered the life out of me, wanting to know if I'd heard anything from you. She seemed to miss you something fierce. The two of you were pretty sweet on each other back in high school, weren't you?"

They were edging into the danger zone. "Yeah." There was no use for it. He had to know. "So who's Bailey sweet on these days?"

"Nobody." Abel's answer came instantly. "Hang on. I'll get a key to the cabin for you." Abel stood and went to rummage in a drawer.

"You sure about that? About Bailey, I mean?"

"Dead sure." Abel shot him a thoughtful glance. "Now that I come to think of it, she's never shown interest in any fellow since you two were hanging around together. Not once in all these years, at least as far as I can remember. You aren't looking to stir up the embers of that old campfire, are you?"

"No." Dan toyed with handle of his coffee cup. "Way too much water under the bridge for that. Just curious, is all." He spoke evenly, but it took some effort. "A smart, pretty woman like Bailey Quinn…seems strange that she hasn't settled on somebody."

"Not so strange. Bailey's got an independent streak a mile wide, and she keeps herself too busy for dating. She's never happy unless she's got herself neck-deep in some project. The more hopeless it is, the better she likes it. Come to think of it," Abel added with a wink, "that could explain why she took you on."

Probably more truth in that little joke than Abel realized. "What's she got going on nowadays?"

"For the past few years she's been all about that grocery store of hers. She's finally got it up and running, but now she's bought herself the Perrys' old farm to fix up. That place is in such bad shape, it's going to take a passel of time and hard work, so it's right up Bailey's alley." Abel shrugged and resumed shuffling items around in the drawer.

"What would a single woman want with a broken-down farm?"

"Well, Bailey's real softhearted about little ones, and she never got around to having a family of her own. Emily tells me that once Bailey gets the house fixed up, she's looking into being a foster mom. She's aiming to take in some kids who've had a hard time and give them a good home."

"Is that a fact?" Dan's heart stirred. That sounded like Bailey.

"Yes. It's going to take some doing. She told Emily they just about count the fillings in your teeth before they'll let you into the program. They check out your background and do a safety inspection, all that stuff. That farmhouse is going to need a lot of overhauling before it'll pass muster. I plan on helping her as much as I can, but between the twins, the farm and my carving business, I don't have much free time these days. Here it is!" Abel withdrew a key from the drawer and tossed it to Dan. "This'll open the front and back doors, and it's yours to keep. The cabin will be waiting for you to use whenever you feel like it."

"That's good of you, Abel." Dan weighed the key in his hand as he mulled over what Abel had told him.

So that's why Bailey had finally decided to deal with their situation. She needed a clear ending to their marriage so she could be approved to take in some foster kids.

Plenty of years had come and gone since Bailey had first caught his eye, but one thing hadn't changed. This woman he'd hurt so badly was still one of the nicest people he'd ever met.

Over the years, his regrets about Bailey had dogged him, aching off and on like the knee he'd busted during an ill-advised bull-riding experiment. He'd like to be shed of that pain and guilt. As he'd driven here, he'd found himself hoping Bailey needed a favor, something really big. Something he could do for her so he could leave Pine Valley feeling as if he'd made up for at least some of the pain he'd caused her.

Something a lot more than just a signature on divorce papers.

And from what Abel had just told him, Bailey *did* need help—a lot of it. She had no intention of asking Dan for it, but that didn't mean he couldn't make the offer.

"Dan?"

Belatedly he realized Abel had been talking to him. "Sorry. I zoned out there for a minute. What?"

"I was just saying, you should run by and see Bailey while you're in town. Tomorrow, maybe. She's always at that store of hers by eight thirty. You could surprise her."

"I might do that."

Abel chuckled. "That'll be something, won't it? You walking right in after all these years? Bailey's a hard girl to fluster, but that ought to do it. I can just see her face!"

Dan managed a tight smile. He could, too.

In fact, for the last few hours he hadn't been able to see much of anything else.

At eight o'clock the next morning, Bailey was in her store on her hands and knees chasing a rolling tangerine.

"Gotcha!" she muttered as her fingers closed around the runaway fruit. Then, *"Ow!"*

She'd absentmindedly lifted her head too soon, butting hard against the underside of the wooden table. She carefully backed the rest of the way out, before sitting up to massage her throbbing head.

This was getting ridiculous. Seeing Dan yesterday had really rattled her. So far this morning she'd broken a jar of spaghetti sauce, spilled her coffee on a stack of mail and dropped three pieces of fruit. She hadn't even opened the store yet, and she already wanted to go home.

"You okay?" a male voice called from her storeroom.

Oh, brother. "I'm fine!" Bailey answered quickly.

Lyle York, hands down her least favorite delivery man, poked his greasy head through the storeroom doorway.

"You sure? I could come help you if you want."

"No, thanks." Bailey spoke firmly as she got to her feet. "Everything's under control."

"Why don't you come help me unload this fruit then? It'd go a lot faster if we worked together." He winked suggestively. "It'd be a lot more fun, too."

Ick. Bailey suppressed a shudder. "Sorry. You'll have to handle it by yourself. I'm busy."

Lyle's eyes narrowed. "You don't look so busy to me, but fine. Be that way."

As the deliveryman sulked back into the storeroom, Bailey placed the rescued tangerine with the others in the tempting basket she'd angled on her front table. Just as she reached into the cardboard box for another one, a loud crash came from her storage room.

"Whoops," Lyle called, his voice heavy with sarcasm. "*Sorry.* That crate slipped right out of my hands."

Bailey ground her teeth and stayed silent. Lyle was a pain in the neck, and his efforts to flirt with her were getting more and more annoying. If he wasn't the grandson of the most reliable citrus supplier she'd ever found, she wouldn't have put up with him this long. The man just kept getting pushier, and soon she was going to have to set him back on his heels, no matter how that impacted her fruit deliveries.

But she wasn't feeling up to having that confrontation today. When Dan Whitlock had shown up yesterday afternoon, he'd thrown her so far off balance that she still felt unsteady.

After Dan had left, she'd tried to keep working on the fence, but after a frustrating hour, she'd abandoned the project. She couldn't focus. She couldn't do anything but think about Dan, replaying every snippet of their short conversation over and over again.

It was infuriating. This wasn't who she was, not anymore. The Bailey Quinn who'd been irresistibly drawn to creamy chocolate, greasy French fries and equally bad-for-you guys was long gone. The new and improved Bailey made smart decisions. She ate more kale, exercised faithfully three times a week and preferred do-it-yourself projects to guys with broody eyes, stubborn jaws…and cowboy hats.

It was just that Dan's visit had come at the worst possible time. She'd been feeling restless for a while now. For years she'd poured herself into Bailey's, and now the store was finally flourishing. She was proud of what she'd accomplished, but she needed a new challenge to tackle.

That shouldn't be a problem. According to Jillian, there were plenty of kids needing foster homes—kids who'd suck up every ounce of restless energy Bailey had. All Bailey had to do was get her mistake of a marriage taken care of and find some way to afford the necessary repairs around the farmhouse. Granted, that last part had her stymied, but she'd figure something out. She always did.

But she couldn't afford to get distracted.

Bailey pushed Dan to the back of her mind and returned her focus to the job at hand. Freshly in from Florida, these tangerines would add a nice splash of color to the front of her store. More importantly, they were organically grown and chock-full of vitamin C. In midwinter, these little gems were worth their weight in gold, but maybe she'd run a nice sale on them as a treat for her customers.

If so, she might need to make a bigger display, because they'd be likely to sell out quickly. She had several matching baskets in the storeroom, but she had no intention of venturing back there until after Lyle left. Maybe there was a stray basket stowed behind the checkout counter.

While she was rummaging, there was a knock on the door. Annoyed, Bailey glanced up at the old library clock ticking on the back wall. It wasn't time to open yet, but she'd go ahead and unlock the door. Folks frequently needed to zip in and grab a few things on their way to work, and she had to keep her customers happy.

Bailey took a deep breath and forced a smile—which lasted until the moment she saw who was waiting outside on the sidewalk.

What was Dan doing here? Her pulse sped up, and Bailey bit down sharply on the tender inside of her lower lip.

This couldn't be good.

She rounded the wooden counter, crossed briskly to the door and unlatched it. It took a minute—the lock was always tricky. Although she deliberately kept her eyes focused on the fussy mechanism, she was very aware of Dan standing just on the other side of the glass. In spite of her better judgment, she looked up and met his eyes as she slid the bolt free.

He was looking right at her, so close that his breath misted the glass between them. For a second, their eyes locked, and her heart gave a painful thump. She looked away and jerked the door open, too flustered to bother with courtesy.

"What are you doing here, Dan?"

He lifted an eyebrow at her tone. "Good morning to you, too."

"Sorry. It's just… I'm really busy right now."

He nodded. "Yeah, I heard you're doing really good with this place." As Dan's eyes left hers to skim the store, Bailey felt a little of her confidence return in spite of her skittering nerves.

Bailey's was as close to perfect as she could make it. The store's trademark decor was an eclectic mix of old and new, and she'd chosen each feature with care. She'd replaced the broken antique lights with retro re-creations, and she'd splurged on the best heating and air unit she could afford. But she'd restored the wide pine floorboards, even though replacing them would have been cheaper. She'd even paid extra to have them refinished in a way that had showcased their interesting scarring.

She'd spent happy weekends combing estate sales and antique stores for the primitive cabinets lining the walls. The jams and sauces displayed on their shelves were made using her own unique recipes, and she'd designed the brick-red logo on their labels herself. Everything in this space bore her personal touch—literally. She'd spent a few weeks three summers ago with oddly colored fingers after chalk painting the farmhouse tables she used to showcase baskets of fresh fruit and vegetables.

She missed those days. Fixing up a store was a lot more fun than running one.

"It looks like something out of a magazine." Dan had pulled his hat off his head and was running it around in his hands again. "Sorry, I don't mean to keep you from your work. I just wanted you to know that after I left your place, I went by to see Abel."

"Did you?" In spite of her irritation, Bailey was curious. "How'd that go?"

"Better than I deserved." Dan's surprisingly humble answer came back without hesitation. Like that cowboy hat he kept playing with, this humility was something new.

Which meant Bailey wasn't quite sure how to respond to it.

"Your brother's a good man."

"He is that. He invited me to stay in the old cabin for a few days. Spend some time getting to know his family and all. No—" Dan held up a hand when Bailey opened her mouth. "Don't worry. Abel thinks I've come back just to see him, and I haven't told him any different. I'm not planning to cause you any trouble. In fact, I think I've come up with a way I could be some help to you, if you'll let me."

"Help?" Bailey wrinkled her forehead. "What kind of help are you talking about?"

"That's going to take a little explaining, and I expect you'll have customers coming along shortly. Why don't you drive out to the cabin this evening for a few minutes? That way we can talk things over, just you and me."

Just you and me. The thrill she felt at Dan's words only made Bailey's inner alarm system clang louder. Bad idea, spending time alone with this man, any way you sliced it.

But oh, she wanted to. She wanted to go to that cabin so much it almost scared her. She wanted to sit down and listen to whatever Dan wanted to say. She wanted to *look* at him, to remind herself of past moments that she'd be far better off forgetting.

This wasn't good. The man had been in town less than twenty-four hours, and she was already flip-flopping like a hooked sunfish.

"Fruit's unloaded, Bailey." Lyle poked his head back through the doorway. "Now how about being a sweet-heart and fixing me some coffee before I head out? I got more deliveries up around Atlanta. That traffic's killer, and I need to be alert."

Bailey threw him an irritated look. She'd offered Lyle a cup of coffee exactly once, when he'd used fatigue as an excuse for banging his truck into the concrete loading dock at the rear of the store. He'd taken the opportunity to sit too close to her and make skeevy comments about how great her hair smelled. She didn't have the time or energy for Lyle's nonsense this morning.

"Sorry. I don't have any coffee made. You could stop by the church coffee shop and get some if you want. They should be open by now. Drive safe, and give your grandpa my best."

Lyle's expression darkened. He darted a wary glance at Dan. "Before I leave, you better at least come back here and take a look at how I got this fruit stacked up. You know how picky you are about that, and besides, we haven't had any chance to talk since I got here."

Bailey frowned, but before she could reply, Dan cut in.

"I believe the lady said you could go." His voice was calm, but there was a steely undertone in it that made the hairs on the back of Bailey's neck tickle, the way they did when lightning was about to strike.

Lyle opened his mouth to protest, but then his narrowed eyes scanned Dan from head to toe. The pace of the delivery man's gum chewing picked up nervously, and he held up both hands in a conciliatory gesture. "Hold your horses there, Tex. I don't see how this is any of your business, but fine. Have it your way, Bailey, but you better not go complaining to Pops if you end up having to move those heavy crates around by yourself. I'll stop back by on my way home in a couple of days and see if you got any additions to your order. Maybe by then you'll be in a better mood."

Bailey ignored him. She waited until she heard Lyle slam the loading door before she spoke again. "Dan—"

Dan interrupted her, his eyes still focused on the back of the store. "That guy's trouble, Bailey. You should make sure you have somebody else in the store with you when he comes back by."

"*Lyle?* He's annoying, sure, and I obviously need to set him straight about a couple things. But, trust me, he's harmless."

"I don't think so. I've worked with a lot of different kinds of men on the ranch, and I've run across a few like him. A man like that's going to try something, sooner or later."

"I doubt that, but if he does, I'll handle it. I'm not the same girl you knew back in high school, Dan. I've gotten pretty good at looking after myself." Bailey let the pointed words settle between them for a second. Then she opened her mouth to nix the whole cabin conversation idea in no uncertain terms. Whatever Dan had to say to her, he could say right here and right now or not at all. "Look, I'm sorry, but—"

But before she got any farther, the shop bell chimed.

Bailey's heart dropped as Jillian Marshall came into the store.

The sharp-eyed redhead was the last person Bailey wanted to see right now. She and Jillian were friendly enough, but Jillian was also Pine Valley's senior social worker. When it came to her job, she was a professional all the way down to her cute ankle-high boots. Bailey didn't have a clue what Dan wanted to talk to her about, and she didn't want to jeopardize her foster parent application by having that conversation in front of Jillian.

"I'm so glad you're open early, Bailey! You've saved my life. One of the social workers in the office has a birthday today, and I totally forgot it was my turn to bring the goodies."

As Jillian headed for the baked goods, Bailey turned back to Dan and spoke in a low voice. "All right. I'll stop by the cabin after work. Say around seven? But I won't be able to stay long."

"That'll be fine. I'll see you then." He flashed an easy smile that effectively stopped her heart. Then he settled his hat back on his head and started for the door. Bailey watched him go.

No man who was as much trouble as Dan Whitlock should be that good-looking. It wasn't fair.

"Bailey?" She jumped and turned to see Jillian holding up two packages of cookies with a confused expression. "I think you'd better come help me. I left my reading glasses at home, and I've been making a mess of everything all morning."

Bailey sneaked another glance at Dan's retreating shoulders and sighed. "You're not the only one," she muttered.

* * *

A few minutes before seven that evening, Bailey nosed her protesting truck up the driveway to the old Whitlock cabin. She hadn't been up this way in a while, and she'd forgotten how steep this driveway was.

"I know how you feel, Maude," she said, patting the sputtering pickup on its faded dashboard. "But we'll survive this, both of us."

At least she hoped so.

As she pulled the keys from the ignition, Dan stepped out onto the cabin's high front porch. "I heard you coming from the time you turned off the county road," he called as she got out. "You might need to get that engine checked over."

"No worries. Maude likes to kick up a fuss, but she never lets me down." Bailey climbed the wooden porch steps. Determined to act cool, collected and perfectly normal, she held out a polite hand as soon as she was within arm's length.

Dan swiped his own hand on his jeans before accepting hers. "Sorry, my hand's pretty sweaty. Being back here at this cabin's making me squirrelly."

Small wonder. Bailey squeezed his hand a little more warmly than she'd originally intended. It couldn't be easy for Dan, coming back to this house. He'd been miserable here.

"The cabin's different, though," she pointed out gently. This property had been an unkempt, trash-littered wreck back in the day. Dan and Abel's father had spent what little money he managed to cadge or steal on liquor, not home maintenance. When Abel had inherited the cabin, he'd set about transforming it in his slow and steady way. "Anybody would be proud to call this place home now."

"Not me. If I were Abel, I'd have bulldozed it to the ground." Dan looked around, his lips tight, then shrugged and pushed open the door. "But you're right. It does look a lot better than it used to. Come on in and see for yourself."

Actually, Bailey had visited the restored cabin before, but now, a new homeowner herself, she looked around with a sharpened interest. She was always prospecting for ideas, and this living room had exactly the feel she loved best. Welcoming, simple and warm.

The knotty pine floor gleamed. The fireplace, made of smooth river stones, sheltered a small, crackling fire, and the oversize furniture angled around the hearth was comfortable and unpretentious. The room had a masculine feel leftover from Abel's bachelor days, but Emily had added a few feminine touches here and there. An old-fashioned braided oval rug brought red and turquoise notes to the room. The attractive colors were echoed by some throw pillows and a snuggly looking afghan tossed over the back of the leather sofa. Some of Abel's wood carvings were displayed on the built-in bookshelves, with small lights carefully angled to showcase their delicate details.

That would be Emily's doing, too. She was fiercely proud of her husband's incredible talent, while he tended to downplay it.

Bailey crossed the room under the pretext of warming her hands at the fire, but really she just needed to put a buffering distance between herself and Dan. Whenever he was close by, Bailey caught a whiff of seasoned leather mixed with fresh cedar. That particular smell was something she'd always associated with Dan, and it was making it really hard for her to think.

And way too easy for her to remember.

Bailey never allowed herself to dwell on the weekend they'd run away together. Some scars were best left unpoked. But being here with Dan, inhaling his scent, brought it all flooding back.

She'd been so excited that Friday night, riding in the middle of his truck's bench seat, cuddled against him as he drove north under the stars. When they'd rolled past the Tennessee state line, she remembered, he'd looked down at her.

"You're not scared, are you, Bailey?"

"Not a bit," she'd assured him. "Not while I'm with you."

But of course she'd been scared. With strict parents like hers, running away was no joke. And getting married at eighteen…well, that brought up plenty of other things to feel nervous about.

When Dan had taken her hands in the secluded corner of her parents' backyard and asked her to elope, he'd seen her hesitation. And she'd seen the surprised hurt on his face, seen the defiant way he'd set his jaw. He was leaving town with her or without her, he'd said. He loved her, and if she wanted to stay here with her parents, he understood. But she was going to have to make her choice.

And so she'd agreed to his plan, confident that once they were married, she'd be able to talk him into coming back and making peace with her parents. Dan always did what she asked sooner or later. And as his wife, she'd have even more leverage.

Turned out she hadn't known Dan nearly as well as she'd thought.

After their quickie wedding, she'd broached the subject of returning home and facing her family, and he'd stared at her as if she'd lost her mind.

"I'm your husband now, Bailey. We're a family, just the two of us. Aren't we? That means our home can be anywhere we want it to be. Just as long as we're together." They'd argued for hours, and then he'd stormed out.

Waiting alone in the shabby motel room, she'd studied the cheap gold band on her finger through her frustrated tears and finally realized the full gravity of the choice she'd made.

Things had only gotten worse from there. When Dan hadn't reappeared by the next morning, she'd taken all the money in her purse and hired a taxi back home, told her worried parents a lie and waited for him to show up. Surely he'd come back for her. After all, they were married.

But weeks, then months had ticked by, and Dan had never come back.

Until now.

That brokenhearted girl who'd peered so hopefully through her mother's living room curtains had learned a few things since then, and Bailey had enough sense to know that she was revisiting some dangerous territory.

"I can make a pot of coffee if you want," Dan was saying.

Bailey shook her head. "No, thanks. I really can't stay long. In fact, you'd best just go on and say whatever it is that you wanted to say to me."

He looked uneasy, but he nodded. "All right. Abel

told me you're working to get your place fixed up so that you can take in some kids who need homes. I thought while I was here maybe I could help you out with that. Working on a ranch for the last ten years has taught me how to fix pretty much anything. I run a good, straight fence line, too." He offered her that slow smile that always made her stomach shift. "Judging by what I saw yesterday, you could use some help that department."

Bailey shot him a narrow look. "For crying out loud, Dan, I wasn't doing *that* bad."

"Not for a newbie, I'll give you that. Anyhow, I've got a little time to spare, and Abel wants me to get to know the kids and all. But he won't want me underfoot all the time, and I sure don't want to hang around this cabin. Seems like a no-brainer to me."

Bailey stared at him. She knew perfectly well this was a crazy idea, but he made it sound so sensible. And free skilled labor? Wasn't that just what she'd been praying for?

But still.

Lord, I'm honestly not sure what to do here. Is this really Your answer? Dan Whitlock?

"So?" Dan prodded. "What do you say?" When she didn't respond, he went on earnestly, "I know you've got your reasons for wanting to keep your distance, and I don't blame you. But just from what I saw out at your place, you've got a lot of work to do. I came back here with an eye toward making things right between us, so I'd really like to help you out. Besides, you know the kind of home I grew up in, how bad it was. If you're trying to take kids out of places like that, I'd consider it an honor to be a part of what you're doing." He waited a second and then added gruffly, "I know we're over, Bailey. But let me end things right this time. Please."

That half-shamed *please* did her in. She sighed. "If you really want to help, I guess… I guess we could give it a try."

Dan's eyes lit up. "Great! I know you're in a hurry, but how about we sit down for just a minute so you can tell me what all you're looking to do? Abel's sure to have some paper stashed around her someplace. I'll find it, and we'll make a list of everything you need done. It won't take a minute." As he disappeared in search of the paper, he called over his shoulder, "You won't be sorry, Bailey, I give you my word. Anyway, what have you got to lose?"

"The same thing I lost last time you gave me your word," Bailey mumbled when she was sure he was well out of earshot. "Everything."

Chapter Four

Bailey pulled back the edge of her living room curtain. The dawn had barely begun to turn the edges of the sky pink, but Dan was already pulling up in her driveway. She cupped her hands around her mug of steaming coffee and watched as he got out of the truck, retrieved a box of tools from the bed and headed toward the house.

He was wearing a sheepskin-lined vest over a plaid shirt and jeans today. And that ever-present cowboy hat, a constant reminder that Dan didn't belong in Pine Valley, Georgia, anymore.

Not that he ever had, no matter how much she'd wanted him to.

She opened the door just as he reached her porch. "You're here early."

He set the toolbox beside the door and gestured toward the brightening light behind him. "Sun's up. Back on the ranch, that means it's time to get to work. Besides, I hoped if I came over early enough, you'd have time to walk the fence line with me and show me exactly where you want it run." He skimmed a glance around her shabby living room and raised an eyebrow. "You sure you want me to start with the fencing? No offense, but this house needs a good bit of work."

"I know, but the fence is a priority. I have to block off the pond for the safety inspection, and I'd like to get it done while the weather's cooperating." Besides, having Dan work outside felt a lot less intimate than letting him work inside her home.

"You're the boss." He glanced down at her feet. "Do you have time to show me where you want the posts set or not? If you do, you'll need to ditch those heels."

He had a point. She'd dressed for work and for the visit to the lawyer's office afterward. The shoes she'd chosen weren't made for trekking through damp pastures. "I think so. The area I want fenced isn't very big, so it won't take long. Go help yourself to some coffee while I swap shoes."

"That sounds good. Thanks." He smiled his slow smile, and Bailey's pulse thumped its standard response.

As she headed up the creaking staircase, she practiced taking deep, calming breaths. If Dan was going to be hanging around, she couldn't keep going all jittery every time the man looked at her.

She switched to a pair of scuffed leather hiking boots and clumped back down the stairs to find Dan waiting in the living room, holding a coffee mug.

"You good to go?"

When she nodded, he opened the door with his free hand, gesturing for her to step through. She walked into the bracing January air.

"Chilly today," she remarked as they headed for the garden area.

His laugh puffed into a coffee-scented mist. "If you say so."

"I do." Bailey made a face at him. "But I guess you're all toughened up from living in the frozen north."

"Not so north and not so frozen, just a lot colder than this. More open, too." He glanced at the pines around them. "I forgot how many trees there are around here. And the smell of them—of these particular pines, I mean—takes me back."

Judging by the tone of his voice, the place that piney scent took him wasn't someplace he wanted to go. Bailey felt a little stung. "Your time in Georgia wasn't all bad, Dan. Was it?"

He glanced at her, and their eyes met. And for a second there, the memories that glimmered between them in the frosty air seemed almost as visible as the clouds of their breath.

"No," he finally said, softly. "Not all bad."

Bailey felt her lips tipping upward, and her internal alarm system pinged. What was she doing? They hadn't even made it to the fence line yet, and she was already bringing up the past, dabbling her toes in dangerous waters. It was going to take them at least fifteen minutes to walk around the little area she needed enclosed. Who knew what they'd end up talking about?

She needed a distraction.

Abruptly she broke away and headed for the barn. "Wait here a second," she called over her shoulder.

Once in the barn, she went for Lucy Ball's stall. The gate leading into the small back pasture was open, but the long-legged calf was still inside finishing her breakfast. She looked up curiously as Bailey approached, crumbs of grain clinging to her damp black nose.

"Feel like a walk, Lucy?" It was a rhetorical question. Lucy always felt like a walk when it meant she got to kick up her hooves on the wrong side of her fence. Bailey unlatched the gate, and the calf gamboled past her and out into the sunshine.

Dan was drinking his coffee, his head angled toward the sun peeking through the fringes of the dark green pine needles. When he saw the calf trotting in his direction, he lifted an eyebrow.

"Got an escapee?"

"This is Lucy Ball. She likes to go for walks."

"You mean, like a dog?" Dan shook his head ruefully. He held out one hand, and the inquisitive calf came up slowly. He wiggled a finger, and she licked it with her wide pink tongue. "She's a nice-looking calf. One of Abel's?"

"Yes, she was a farm-warming gift. Did they tell you?"

Dan laughed. "I've been working on a ranch for ten years, Bailey. I may not know much else, but cattle I know. This one has the same lines as that old milk cow out at Goosefeather."

Lucy pranced off toward the pond, and Bailey and Dan fell in step behind her. "This ranch you keep talking about. You like working there?"

Dan hesitated before answering. "I like the work. It's simple. Clear cut." He chuckled. "Hard. I came to it when I needed that kind of life, and it made a big difference for me. Well, that and the people I met there. Gordon McAllister owned the ranch, and his grandson, Colt, worked on it during the summers. They got to be like family to me."

"Oh?" Bailey kicked at a small stone. It skittered through the frosted grass, making Lucy Ball shy to the side. So Dan had found himself a new family out west. As if he hadn't had anybody back home waiting for him. Worrying about what might have happened to him. "How'd you meet them?"

"I hired on as a seasonal hand when I was at a pretty low point. My drinking was out of control by then, and it wasn't long before it caught up with me. I totaled one of the ranch trucks driving drunk. Instead of firing me like I expected, Gordon bailed me out on his own dime. He gave me a chewing out I deserved and a second chance I didn't. It came with conditions, like going to AA and attending church with him every Sunday. I slipped up a couple more times, but Gordon never gave up on me. He believed I had the makings of a decent human being, and finally I decided maybe he was right."

His use of the past tense and the sadness in his voice clued Bailey in. "He's not…with you anymore?"

"Gordon passed on about a year ago." Dan inhaled deeply. "Colt and his wife, Angie, run the Bar M now."

"I'm sorry, Dan. Both my parents are gone now, too. When you lose people who've meant that much to you, it's really hard."

"Yeah. It is."

"But you still work on the ranch?"

He shot her a quick sideways glance. "For now. So, you'll want the fence to turn here and cut in front of the tree line?"

"Yes." She waited as Dan broke off a branch and

rammed it into the ground. For the next few minutes, they crunched along on the fragrant pine needles without talking.

When they reached the third turn, Dan stuck in another branch one-handed. Then he took a last swallow of coffee before dumping the dregs out on the ground. He stood for a minute, looking over the scene in front of them.

The small round pond glittered under the blue sky, and in the distance the dilapidated farmhouse nestled among its overgrown azalea bushes. Those were still winter bare, but an optimistic forsythia bush was putting out tiny glowing buds of bright yellow beside the front porch. If it didn't freeze in the next cold snap, at least she'd have one pretty thing to look at until spring got here.

Bailey darted a quick look up into Dan's face. "Go ahead and say it. The place looks awful."

He shrugged. "It needs fixing, that's all. Other than that, it's nice. Some houses just look like houses. But this place looks like it could be a home."

Funny. That was exactly what she'd said when the real estate agent had brought her here. *It looks like home.* "Yeah, but it'll take a lot of work."

"Anything worth having takes work." He met her eyes and winked. "Another thing ranching taught me, I guess."

"How big is the ranch you work on?" she asked as they resumed their trek around the fence line.

"The Bar M? A shade over twelve hundred acres."

Bailey's mouth dropped open. "I thought this place was huge, and it's only twenty-six acres including the house lot!" She shook her head slowly. "Twelve hundred acres!"

"Size isn't everything. I'm just the foreman at the Bar M, but this place is all yours, Bailey. That counts for a lot. Besides—" his greenish-brown eyes twinkled "—you wouldn't want to buy fencing for a twelve-hundred-acre spread, would you?"

"No, I guess not. Speaking of fencing—" Bailey gestured toward the heap of fencing materials piled close to the house. "That's what I have to work with. Abel had some leftover wire and posts, and he let me have them. You'll have to set the wire close enough that a child couldn't slip through. I hope it'll be enough to go around."

Dan's eyes skimmed the stack. "Should be. You know, it's a really great thing you're doing, Bailey, taking in kids who need a home. Not that I'm surprised. You're a good person. Even back in high school, you were always looking for somebody to help."

Her heart swelled at his praise, and she tried to hide her reaction by taking a sip of her cold coffee before replying. "You're the one helping me right now, Dan, and I appreciate it. I want you to know that."

"I'm glad to do it." Dan looked down at her, and the gentleness in his eyes hit her with the forceful jolt of a bittersweet memory. He'd always looked at her like that. But only her. He'd viewed pretty much everybody else with a chilly suspicion that had come across as a sullen defiance. But whenever he'd turned those hard eyes in her direction, they had instantly softened. It had made her feel… "Special," he was saying, and for a second, she was afraid she'd spoken her thoughts aloud.

"Wh-what?"

"You're special to me. I know our past has its black marks, believe me, but I just want you to know, even after the divorce is final—if you ever need me, all you have to do is call."

"That's nice of you."

Their eyes held, and the moment stretched out a fraction of a second too long.

Bailey could feel the heat rising into her cheeks. She dropped her gaze and looked at her watch.

"I'd better get to work. I'm leaving the house unlocked for you. Bathroom's the third door on the left down the hall, and there's a water dispenser in the fridge."

"All right." He nodded at Lucy, who was licking one of the wooden fence posts. "I'll put your calf-puppy back in her pasture, and I'll see you when you get back."

"Thanks!" Bailey started toward the house. She needed to grab her keys and her purse and get on the road. "But you'll probably be gone by the time I get home. I have that appointment with the lawyer after work, so I'll be late."

"I'll be here," he called after her. "Until the light goes, anyway."

Bailey nodded. She glanced down at her wristwatch again as she went up the steps, but the late hour wasn't actually her biggest problem anymore.

That unmistakable little thrill of joy she'd felt at Dan's words was way more worrisome.

I'll be here.

At half past twelve, Dan set down the post-hole diggers and stretched his back. He was just over midway around the perimeter of the fence line. It had been a while since he'd set fence by hand, and he'd forgotten what hard, sweaty work it was.

And Bailey had figured on doing this job all on her own. He had a lot more upper-body strength and experience, and it was still tough going. He didn't see how she could have managed it, but he was impressed by her gumption.

He fished a slightly squashed sandwich out of his toolbox and glanced toward the house. Bailey had said she'd left it open. He could go inside. It would give him a chance to sit down for a few minutes, maybe drink a cold glass of water.

It would also give him a chance to take a closer look at the nest Bailey was making for herself—and get a better idea of the repairs that needed doing.

Dan shed his dirty boots on the front porch and padded sock-footed into the empty house. The place was shabby enough to be an eyesore, but he kind of liked it anyway. It felt peaceful. Something tightly wound inside him uncurled a little.

In a strange way, it reminded him of the ranch house at the Bar M, although the two looked nothing alike. The McAllister home was a sprawling place, well kept and built to handle all the extremes the Wyoming weather would throw at it. And this…well, this place was about two steps up from a dump. But somehow the houses had a similar feel. Maybe because they were both old enough to have their own personalities, like a pair of jeans that were worn enough to fit you just right.

This one needed a ton of work, but that didn't scare him any more than it had scared Bailey. In fact, if things had been different, if he and Bailey had been house hunting together like a regular married couple, he'd have been completely on board with buying this place, warts and all.

He wouldn't have told her that at first, though. He'd have teased her about the place's flaws while she praised its good points. He'd have drawn the argument out, just for the sheer fun of it, but in the end he'd have laughed and picked her up and twirled her right through that big, heavy old front door and—

He broke off the daydream midtwirl. No point going any farther. Might-have-beens were dead ends.

He looked around. The living room was furnished with a comfortable rust-red love seat and an overstuffed chair with a chubby footstool in front of it. The colors had some spark, and nothing looked too spindly to actually sit on. Really pretty but not persnickety.

Just like Bailey. No wonder he liked it.

It had some major issues, though. The walls were horizontal unplastered boards layered with peeling paint, and there was a drop cloth in one corner where Bailey had scraped through at least five colors. There was a suspicious dark splotch on the ceiling that probably led to a leaky spot in the roof, while the second window down the side of the room had a spiderwebbing crack in it.

Making mental notes about the material he'd need to make the repairs, Dan carried his sandwich into the kitchen.

This room needed even more work. The cabinets and flooring were throwbacks to another age. The appliances were new, though. The stove that hunkered in one corner was every bit as massive as the one at the

Bar M, but from the look of its control panel, it sported even more bells and whistles.

Bailey had always loved to cook, and she'd always done a bang-up job of it, too. He had a sudden image of her busy at that stove, her face flushed with warmth. He'd be standing by with the intention of helping her out, but he'd probably just get in her way—and get swatted when he tried to sneak a taste too soon.

He shook his head to clear the appealing picture. He shouldn't have come inside. This place was getting to him. He saw Bailey everywhere he looked.

Maybe she hadn't lived here very long, but her touches were all over the place. The little streaks of paint she'd dabbed onto the old cabinets, testing out the colors. The pot of narcissus blooming in the window, shaking its fist at the winter. They all said *Bailey* to him.

But he hadn't come in here to moon around dreaming silly daydreams. He needed to eat his lunch and get back to work.

He opened one of the sagging cabinets and discovered a cache of clean glasses, neatly upended on clean paper. He grabbed one and headed for the ice dispenser on the fridge.

He stuck it in the little niche, pressing the lever, and as the ice clanked into the glass, his eye was caught by an index card stuck on the front of the appliance.

He squinted and read the words aloud. "'I will lift up mine eyes to the hills, from whence cometh my help. My help comes from the Lord, the maker of heaven and earth.'"

The verse echoed in the stillness of the kitchen. Underneath it she'd written, "The Lord will send me the help I need. Nothing is impossible with God."

A sudden clattering sound woke him up. "Whoa!" He'd forgotten about the ice and his glass had overflowed, bits of ice hitting the peeling linoleum and skittering around. He spent the next minute collecting the frozen shards and tossing them into the chipped porcelain sink, thinking hard.

When he'd cleaned up the mess, he filled his glass carefully with water and settled down at the table with his sandwich in front of him.

He hesitated. He'd come a long way in his faith over the past years, but praying was something that he still found hard sometimes. Finally, he glanced up toward the old-fashioned, grooved board ceiling.

"God? I figured You brought me back here for a reason, but that verse there just clinched it. Looks like Bailey's been praying for some help, and if it's all the same to You, I'd like to ask for the job. The whole job. Not just the fencing." He paused, looking around the shabby room. "Doing the work won't be much of a problem, but talking Bailey into it is going to be a whole different ball game. I'd sure appreciate Your help with that part. Thank You, and amen."

Then he unwrapped his sandwich and took a big bite. He needed to make a trip to town, and he didn't have any time to waste.

Chapter Five

At Banks Building Supply, Dan waited while Myron Banks, the elderly owner, totaled up the cost of the supplies on a chittering adding machine.

"This is a passel of stuff," the old man mumbled, punching keys with gnarled fingers. "Gonna come up to a fair amount." He shot Dan a look from under his bushy white eyebrows. "You sure you got the green to pay for all this, son?"

"Yeah, I can cover it." Dan pulled his wallet out of his jeans pocket. Thumbing through, he lifted out his personal credit card.

Bailey wasn't going to be too happy about him paying for the stuff he needed to get started on the house repairs. But according to the deal he'd just struck, that fell on God's end of things. Dan would focus on doing his part, which meant getting Bailey's place fixed up as best he could in the time he had.

"There." Myron ripped off a strip of curling paper and pushed in Dan's direction. "Told you it was going to be steep, but I gave you a discount 'cause you're buying so much."

"I appreciate that." When Dan offered his credit card, an alarmed look spread over the old man's face.

"Sorry, I got a policy. I don't do no credit cards." He indicated a hand-lettered sign on the back wall—No Credit or Debit Cards. "I don't fool with all that computerized stuff. Folks'll steal you blind, you go putting your money on the internet."

"No problem." Smothering a smile, Dan tucked the card back into his wallet. "I'll write you a check. You got any policies against those?"

The old man looked cautious. "Well now, that depends. What's your name, son?"

Dan pulled out the blank check he always kept in his wallet for emergencies and picked up a pen from the chipped mug on the counter. "Dan Whitlock."

"Whitlock, did you say?"

The change in the man's voice made Dan's spine stiffen. He looked up. Then he dropped the pen back into the mug. He wouldn't be writing any checks in this store.

"That's right."

"Kin to the Whitlocks here, are you?"

"Abel's my brother."

"*He*'s a good man." There was the faintest emphasis on *he*. "You'd be the younger of Elton's boys, I'm reckoning?" When Dan nodded, the man went on. "You buying this stuff for Abel?"

"No, just helping out a friend while I'm in town."

The old man studied the steep figure circled on the adding machine paper. "Out-of-town checks are too chancy for a small operator like me. Cash would do better. You can take your check right over to the bank downtown. They'll cash it for you." *If it's any good.*

The unspoken words hung in the air. The elderly man straightened his thin shoulders resolutely. "I'll hold this material for you until five o'clock this evening. That'll give you time to see to getting a check cashed. After that I'll have to put it back in the stock. That's the best I can do."

"I understand." Dan chewed on the inside of his cheek, but he kept his voice civil. "I'll be back." He picked up his hat from the counter and clapped it on his head.

"No offense meant, son," Myron called after Dan as he left the office area. "Just trying to stay out of trouble, that's all."

"So am I," Dan muttered.

He fumed the entire brief ride to the bank, but he aimed most of the anger at himself. He should've seen this coming a mile off. He'd forgotten where he was—and who he was when he was in Pine Valley. Myron's refusal to accept his check had nothing to do with it being from out of town…and everything to do with the name on it.

Whitlock.

Once he'd been used to the suspicions that clung to that name, but he'd gone away and nearly forgotten. Here in Pine Valley, Whitlock stood for thievery and double dealings. Even Abel's straight-arrow way of doing business couldn't entirely erase the stink of generations of cheats, especially not for an old-timer like Myron Banks.

Especially not when Dan had cheated people more than once himself, back in the day.

Funny. Back in Wyoming, Dan didn't even have to go down to the building supply in person. He just called in what he needed, and they had it delivered. Promptly. As the trusted foreman of the sprawling Bar M and a close friend of the well-respected McAllisters, Dan's name tended to open doors rather than shut them.

But back here in his hometown, a man was too suspicious of him to take his check.

That stung, but it fell into the category of things Dan couldn't change, and he'd learned a long time ago to leave that alone. It was another thing Gordon McAllister had drilled into Dan's brain. A man couldn't control what happened to him, but if he could control himself, well, that went a long way.

Fortunately, it didn't take the bank long to verify that he had the necessary funds in his account. Within fifteen minutes, he was walking out, his wallet thick with bills. As he stepped off the curb beside his parked truck, his eye caught on fluttering green-and-white-striped awnings down the street.

Bailey's store. He paused.

She'd be working now. But since he was already in town, he could stop in and see her. That'd be a natural enough thing to do, wouldn't it? He could buy a soda and talk to her for a minute. He could tell her about how that silly Jersey calf of hers had stolen his second-best hammer and run off with it. That'd be sure to make her laugh.

He loved to hear Bailey laugh.

He hesitated another long minute, and then shrugged, impatient with himself. What was he acting so squirrelly about? He'd stop in the store for a second then go back to the building supply and pick up the materials.

This decided, he left the truck and headed down the narrow sidewalk.

He'd never felt at home in this town, but he had to admit, it was pretty. A lot of these one-horse places were dying out—especially downtown—their old-fashioned town squares abandoned in favor of sprawling shopping centers on the outskirts of town.

But Pine Valley was holding her own. Every one of the stores facing the rosy brick courthouse was occupied, and most seemed to be doing a brisk trade. The businesses all looked neat and attractive, the sidewalks were swept, and the traffic was orderly.

All in all, this was a hardworking, honest little town, a fine place to live and raise a family.

If your last name didn't happen to be Whitlock.

"Danny?"

Emily hurried out of a building with big coffee cups painted on its windows. She was wearing an apron, and she had her hair clubbed up into a sleek bun. To Dan's astonishment, she skipped to him and gave him a warm hug.

"I figured that was you! Hard to miss that hat around here! Are you headed to Bailey's?"

"Yeah, for a minute." He smiled at her. After his wake-up call down at the building supply, Emily's kindness was a welcome change.

"I'm headed there in a few minutes myself." Emily glanced at her watch. "Sometimes she closes up for a few minutes around this time of day so she can grab some lunch and putter around in the storeroom. If her sign's up on the door, just slip through the alley and go in the back. That's what I always do. Listen—I want the two of you to come to dinner Friday night. Nothing fancy—just a beef stew—but we're anxious to spend as much time with you as we can while you're in town. Seven o'clock. Tell Bailey I'm not taking no for an answer! Okay?"

When he nodded, she gave his forearm a quick squeeze. "Wonderful! Now I'd better get back inside. I've got a tray of lemon squares almost ready to come out of the oven. Tell Bailey I'll see her in a bit."

With another friendly smile, Emily vanished into the café. Dan stared after her for a second or two before resuming his walk in the direction of Bailey's store.

His welcome in this town sure went from one extreme to the other. Abel and Emily seemed overjoyed to see him. Bailey was kind but wary, and people like Myron Banks were downright suspicious.

It sort of threw a man off his feet.

He pressed the brass lever on Bailey's door, but it didn't budge. Sure enough, when he glanced up, he saw a small square sign posted in the window.

Temporarily Closed. Will Reopen In… The little adjustable clock was showing a time twenty minutes in the future.

He couldn't wait around out here for twenty minutes. He needed to get back out to the building supply and pick up that material. He hesitated, remembering Emily's breezy instructions.

He wasn't sure it was a good idea for him to go around to the back. He was going to be treading on some pretty thin ice with the house repairs. He didn't need to make matters any worse by bugging Bailey while she was having her lunch.

It was too bad, though. He'd really liked the idea of

dropping in on her. He thought for a minute, then he walked a short way down the sidewalk.

Just as Emily had said, there was a narrow alleyway leading to the loading area behind the stores. Couldn't do any harm to walk through and see if maybe Bailey happened to be out back.

He emerged from the damp, shaded alley into an asphalt parking lot and frowned. A delivery truck emblazoned with a huge orange was butted up to the concrete loading pad at the back of Bailey's store.

Had to be that Lyle fellow stopping by on his return run. The back of Dan's neck crinkled uneasily, and he picked up his pace. Just as he mounted the block steps going up to the deck, he heard Bailey's voice drifting through the half-opened door.

"Lyle, I'm not telling you again. The answer is no."

"Aw, come on. You don't really mean that."

"Yes, I do." Bailey spoke firmly, but her voice shook on the last word, just a little.

Whatever was going on in there had her nervous. Dan's heart turned hard and cold at the same time, and his hands fisted against his jeans.

From somewhere inside a man snickered, but there was no smile on Dan's face as he barreled through the doorway.

It happened so fast, Bailey's brain couldn't catch up. One minute, a smirking Lyle had her cornered against a stack of boxes, pestering her to agree to go out with him. Then in a blink he'd been yanked backward by the collar of his shirt.

Dan backed Lyle flat against the brick wall, his forearm pressing against Lyle's neck. Lyle's eyes were wide, and his mouth flexed open and shut like a landed fish.

"Dan!" Bailey choked out. "What are you doing?"

"Teaching this fellow a vocabulary lesson." Dan spoke quietly, but she could see the taut muscle under the sleeve of his shirt as he kept the other man pinned against the wall. "He seems to have some trouble understanding the word *no*."

"I was just playing around—" Lyle protested, but he choked back into silence as Dan adjusted his hold slightly.

"It's not playing unless both people want to play. Maybe you'd better say it out loud so I'm sure you've got that, Lyle."

"You're crazy! Look, Tex, this is none of your business—" Dan shifted his position again, and the delivery man's argument ended in a wheeze.

"Dan!" Bailey called out worriedly. "Be careful."

"It's all right, Bailey. Almost done here. Go ahead, Lyle. Say it."

"It's not playing unless both people want to play," Lyle mumbled grudgingly.

Instantly Dan released him. Lyle sagged down, massaging his throat, his eyes filled with outrage.

"I could have you arrested for that!"

"Go for it," Dan answered evenly. "Now get, before I think up a few more lessons you need to learn."

Alarm kindled in Lyle's eyes, and he edged farther away. Once he was safely out of Dan's reach, he began to bluster. "Don't worry, I'm going. And I won't be back, either. Just you wait until Pops hears about this, Bailey! You won't be getting any more special treatment, that's for sure!"

"If this is your idea of special treatment, I'm not interested," Bailey retorted. "And trust me, I'll be having a word with your grandfather myself."

Lyle's face darkened. He started to speak, but he darted another look at Dan and headed out the door at a trot. A second later, she heard the truck's engine roar to life.

The knot in her stomach loosened at the sound, and her knees began to shake. She reached out and grabbed a metal shelf to support herself.

"Bailey? Are you okay?"

She swallowed hard. "I'm all right. I don't know why I'm shaking. It wasn't… Lyle was just being obnoxious. He called me back here, and then he kept badgering me about going out with him." She flushed. It sounded silly when you said it out loud, but it hadn't felt silly. When he'd cornered her in the storeroom, there had been something in his eyes… She'd gotten truly spooked there for a minute. She forced herself to take a deep breath. "I'm fine."

"You don't look fine." Dan crossed the room in one stride. Maybe it was because all her nerves were already on high alert, but as he neared, her whole body went into a convulsive shiver. "You need to sit." He dragged a wooden stool over. Taking both her upper arms gently in his hands, he lowered her onto the seat. "Try taking a few deep breaths. It's just adrenaline. You'll settle down in a minute."

"What's going on, Bailey?" Emily stood framed in the large open loading door. Her friend hurried over and draped a protective arm over Bailey's shoulders. "Danny, what happened? Is she hurt?"

"She's had a scare," Dan said quietly.

"What kind of scare?" Emily frowned and glanced over her shoulder. "Does this have anything to do with that truck that just squealed out of here? The driver jumped the curb and almost ran over Trisha Saunders's new Pekingese."

"The fruit delivery guy needed a little lesson in manners, that's all," Dan said. "I don't think he's going to be a problem anymore."

Emily looked from Dan to Bailey. "He scared you?"

"I'm not scared. I'm fine," Bailey stood, frustrated to find that her knees still wobbled under her. She couldn't believe she was acting like such a fragile flower...over *Lyle*. "Thanks, Dan. I appreciate you stepping in, but I'm really okay. Now, did you need something from the store, Emily? You must have, or you wouldn't be here."

"Walnuts," Emily admitted after a second. "I need some walnuts."

"Okay." Bailey's voice was already almost back to normal. Good. "No problem. Come out front with me then, and I'll get you fixed up. I need to grab some water anyway. Dan, you wait here, okay? I imagine you had a reason to stop by, too. I mean, apart from setting Lyle straight. Let me take care of Emily. Then I'll be right back, and we'll talk."

Dan nodded. "Take your time. I'm in no particular hurry."

When she and Emily were in the front area of the store, Emily planted herself in front of Bailey.

"Okay, we're alone. Now, Bailey Quinn, you tell me what happened back there! And don't say *nothing*, because you're as white as a sheet. Honey, did that delivery guy put his hands on you?"

"No. Lyle was being…" Bailey struggled to find the right word. "Inappropriate," she finished finally. In spite of herself, she laughed. "Wow. I sound like somebody's old maid aunt, don't I?"

"Tell me exactly what happened," Emily insisted. As they picked out the nuts Emily needed, Bailey described the incident in the storeroom.

Somehow talking about it helped. By the time she'd finished, her breathing had slowed back down to its usual pace, and her knees had stopped jiggling like jelly.

Unfortunately, the story seemed to have the opposite effect on Emily. Her friend's cheeks were a hot pink, and she was shaking her head.

"That's just awful! When I think what could have happened… What a blessing Danny stopped by when he did!"

Bailey threw a quick look back toward the doorway leading to the storeroom and lowered her voice. "He had Lyle up against the wall before I knew what was happening."

"Good. Abel would have done the same thing," Emily said. "He and Danny must be more alike than I thought."

"Alike?" Nerves made Bailey's laugh a little shaky. "Dan and Abel? Hardly. You wouldn't say that if you'd seen him in that storeroom, Emily. For a second there, I was afraid he was going to hurt more than Lyle's pride."

"But he didn't, did he?" Emily shuddered. "When I was a waitress in Atlanta, I had some run-ins with men like that. I'm glad Danny set that guy straight. And I sure hope it'll change the way people around here see

Danny. You wouldn't believe some of the mean-spirited comments folks have made since they've heard he's back in town!"

"Oh, I'd believe. Trust me."

"That's right." Emily looked at her and lifted her brows. "Abel told me you guys dated for a while back in high school. In fact—" she paused for a second "—he wonders if maybe you're why Danny finally came back to town."

"Oh?" Bailey felt a fresh wave of nervousness. "Why would he think that?" She busied herself weighing out the nuts.

"Just an idea he got from a conversation they had. He hopes there's some truth to it. He'd love for Danny to stick around, and Abel already thinks of you as a sister. If you and Danny got back together—"

Bailey interrupted her. "That's not going to happen, Emily. Will a pound of nuts do you?"

"Better make it two. I'm baking apple-walnut muffins. So you really don't care for Danny anymore? That's a shame. Abel's convinced that Danny still has some pretty strong feelings for you."

Bailey bit her lip as she tipped more shelled walnuts onto her vintage scale. Then she glanced up and met her friend's worried eyes. "I'll always care about Dan, Emily. But it won't go any farther than that. I won't let it."

"But, honey, why not?" Emily's eyes narrowed as she scanned Bailey's face. "Danny's my brother-in-law, Bailey, but you're my best friend. If there's something I need to know about him—"

"There isn't. At least, not now, as near as I can tell." Bailey twisted the top of the full cellophane bag and fastened it with a tie. "But I learned my lesson a long time ago where Dan was concerned."

Emily frowned. "You're the last person I'd expect to hold a person's past against them. Dan's really changed, Bailey. Abel's sure of it."

"I hope so. I really do. But I'm still keeping my distance. You know all that gossip you're hearing? I used to be just as outraged about how people talked about Dan as you are now. But here's what I learned— where there's that much smoke, there's usually fire. I ignored everybody's warnings, and I got burned. Badly. If Dan's turned his life around, I'm truly glad, and I wish him every happiness. But for me, that's as far as it goes. I'm not letting him get close enough to hurt me that much again."

A soft cough from the back of the store made both women stiffen. Bailey turned to see Dan standing in the doorway. One look at his face told her that he'd overheard what she'd said.

Bailey's face flushed. She hadn't meant to hurt his feelings. She was just trying to be as honest with Emily as she could be. But after what had happened in the back room, how Dan had come to her rescue, it must seem pretty ungrateful of her to be talking this way to his sister-in-law.

"I'd best be getting on back, Bailey," he said quietly. "I've got work to do. I'll see you this evening, most likely."

"And I'll see both of you at supper on Friday," Emily inserted quickly. Then she turned to Bailey with a pleading expression. "Abel's just so happy Danny's home, and we're celebrating. We really want you to be there, Bailey. Please. For Abel."

Bailey's heart fell, but she recognized the look on Emily's face. Her friend wasn't going to take no for an answer.

"All right. I guess I'll see you then."

Chapter Six

"Redheads," Dan observed aloud, "sure can be troublesome creatures."

Lucy Ball snorted and tossed her curly topknot. She pranced out of reach, his pliers clenched in her mouth. The calf had been stealing tools for the past half hour, and the contents of his toolbox now littered Bailey's pasture.

Lucy was making a nuisance of herself and slowing him down. He should never have let her out of her stall in the first place. But he figured Bailey would be driving up any minute, and he hoped dealing with a mischievous calf would buy him some time while he figured out how to say what he needed to say.

Or if he should say it at all.

Because, for Dan, at least, everything was different now.

The instant he'd charged through that doorway and seen Bailey backed into a corner, he'd known. The feelings he'd kept tied down and hidden for years had been tugging at their tethers ever since he'd heard about Bailey's phone call, but in that moment, they'd surged up with an unstoppable strength. His whole world had shifted and reformed like one of those little gizmos with the colored bits of glass that made different patterns with every turn. The truth had shone out so clearly it had staggered him.

He didn't want a divorce. He wanted to win Bailey back. She was different now, but she was still the woman he wanted, the only woman he'd ever want.

And he wanted it all. He wanted all those sweet little scenes he'd imagined in her house. He wanted to love this woman, protect her, laugh with her. Raise a family with her. Grow old with her.

Hours had passed since then, but his deep certainty hadn't faded a bit, not even when he'd overheard Bailey telling Emily how she didn't trust him and never would. She had every right to feel that way, and he had no clue how to go about changing her mind. But he knew he had to try.

One thing was for sure. He didn't want to talk about any of this with Bailey until he'd thought it through a little better. He'd be sure to say the wrong thing, and there was way too much at stake for that. So he'd let a calf pester the life out of him for the last hour and a half, just so there'd be something to distract Bailey when she got home.

Apparently, he needn't have bothered. Bailey was running late, and the sun was setting, throwing streamers of orange and pink into the sky behind the dark bristles of the pines. Time to pack up, he realized with a sense of relief. He'd spend some time tonight praying and trying to find some kind of answer in the dog-eared Bible Gordon had given him years ago. Maybe by tomorrow he'd be ready to talk to Bailey.

"Come on, girl." Lucy danced sideways playfully, batting her brown eyes and daring him to chase her. Dan didn't bite. He ignored her and started ambling toward the barn by himself. Just as he'd expected, the calf's curiosity got the better of her. He heard the sound of hooves behind him, and sure enough, she followed him right into the stall, where he gave her a bit of grain and plenty of good, clean hay.

"That'll taste better than those rubber tool handles," he murmured, tousling her red mop of hair. Lucy snorted at him, but she swiped his hand with her grain-encrusted tongue.

Dan left the barn, wiping his sticky hand on the leg of his jeans. He sure wished folks were as easy to understand as animals.

He gathered up the scattered tools as fast as he could, but he wasn't quite quick enough. He was cleaning calf slobber off his pliers when he saw the headlights of Bailey's old truck bouncing up the driveway.

His mouth went dry, but he squared his shoulders and stood by the fence line to wait. If he hadn't been watching for it, he'd have missed Bailey's brief hesitation before she headed in his direction. For the first time, it occurred to him that she might have run late on purpose, that maybe he wasn't the only one nervous about this.

Bailey scanned his work in the dimming light and gave him a tense smile.

"Well, you were right. You can run a better fence line than I can. Quicker, too. I can't believe how much you got done in just one day." The admiration in her voice made his sore muscles worth it.

"I've had plenty of practice." Together they surveyed

the long row of fence posts marching into the trees. "Light's gone now, though. I was just about to leave."

Bailey kept her gaze focused on the fence. "I figured you'd already be gone. I had to wait nearly an hour at the lawyer's office. Mr. Monroe's going to draw up the papers for us, but he's got a lot going on right now. It's going to take him a while—he said maybe a couple of weeks. Are you planning to stay in town that long?"

Dan's heart thumped painfully. "About that," he started.

"Dan?" She broke in, her voice puzzled. "What's all that stuff on the porch?" He winced. Her eye had caught on the large stack of Sheetrock and other materials he'd unloaded a few hours earlier.

"I stopped by the building supply in town." He wished he hadn't jumped the gun and put Lucy Ball back in her stall. "By the way, I let that calf of yours out to run a little while. You're going to have your work cut out when you start training her to milk, I'll tell you that much. She's got a personality the size of Texas, and she's already spoiled rotten."

"Dan." There was a dangerous tone in Bailey's voice. "You were just supposed to help me with the fence, remember?" She squinted at the porch. "I see a couple of windows and some siding and a bunch of other stuff up there."

"We said I'd *start* with the fence. The house repairs have to be done, and it's a lot easier to have everything on site so I don't waste time running back and forth to town."

Even in the fading light, he could see the worried creases on her forehead. "I understand, but I'm on a tight budget, Dan. You really shouldn't have bought all that without checking with me first."

"Don't worry about that. It's on me." He saw her face change, and he rushed on, "Look, I heard what you said to Emily. I get that you've got good reasons for keeping your distance, and I don't blame you. But I'd really like to take care of this for you, and I hope you'll let me."

Bailey chewed on her lip for a second. Then she sighed. "I guess we'd better have a talk. When you're done getting your tools together, please come on inside." She turned away and walked toward the house.

Dan watched her go with a sinking feeling. Looked like they were having this conversation now, ready or not. He hoped he wouldn't blow it.

By the time Dan had gathered his tools and stowed the toolbox in the bed of his truck, it was almost fully dark. Bailey had flipped on the living room lamp, and a warm square of bright yellow lit up the front porch. The welcoming golden light made the gathering darkness surrounding him seem even colder and blacker.

It put him in mind of his first few months on the ranch. He and the other hands would work until dark. They'd all come riding up, tired to the bone, and they'd see the ranch house lights glimmering over the hill. At the time, that light had meant food and a safe place to sleep. Those had been pretty valuable commodities for him back then, and he'd been thankful for them. For a long time, the ranch had been the closest thing to a home he'd ever known.

But even back then he'd never felt the same pull he felt now, and he knew why. Bailey hadn't been there, waiting inside. And he was starting to understand that home for him was wherever Bailey Quinn happened to be.

Even when she was ready to chew off a strip of his hide.

Bailey met him at the door. She wasn't smiling, but she held out a mug of steaming coffee. "Here. I figured you might be chilly. It's decaf, so it won't keep you from sleeping."

"Thanks." He accepted the mug, cupping his hands around the warmth. Back in Wyoming he drank fully leaded coffee around the clock, and it had never stopped him from sleeping whenever he had the chance. Caffeine was no match for long hours of ranch work. But at least Bailey cared about whether or not he slept. That was encouraging.

"Let's sit down. I have a couple of things I'd like to say to you."

"Sure." Dan lowered himself onto the overstuffed chair. Bailey settled on the sofa, tucking one leg under herself.

She drew in a breath and looked him in the eye. "First off, I want to thank you again for helping me out with Lyle today. Apparently I misjudged him, and I'm really grateful you came in when you did."

"You're welcome. And don't beat yourself up for not taking Lyle's measure right off. I've been fooled by a few like him myself."

Bailey's fingernails tapped the side of her mug. "I'm sorry about what I said to Emily. I was…flustered. But that's no excuse. You've gone out of your way to be kind and helpful ever since I called you. It wasn't tactful of me to say all that, especially not to your brother's wife."

It wasn't *tactful* of her to say she didn't trust him. Not it wasn't *true*.

"You were just being honest." He took a breath. "More honest than you've been with me. You keep saying you've gotten past what happened between us, but it's pretty clear you haven't, not really."

"I've forgiven you." Bailey looked exasperated, and there was a tired vertical line between her dark brows. "But that doesn't change the fact that you still scare the life out of me."

He could actually feel the color draining out of his cheeks. "Bailey, you have to know that I'd never hurt you." Belatedly he realized how stupid that statement must sound to the woman he'd already hurt so badly. He opened his mouth to explain, but she shook her head.

"That's not what I meant. Look, you seem to have turned your life around, and I give you a lot of credit for that. But it's just—for me, you're like chocolate. Remember how much I always loved chocolate? I've been eating healthy for years, but if you put a box of chocolates in front of me right this minute, I'd struggle not to eat them all. Even though I've worked really hard to shed those extra pounds. Even though I know better. Do you understand?"

He understood, all right. She was saying that he was bad for her.

"Yeah. I do."

"Good." Bailey looked relieved. "Anyway, like I said, the divorce papers will be ready before long, and then you'll be going back to Wyoming."

The words came out before he could stop them. "Maybe not."

"What do you mean?"

Dan hesitated, but it was too late to back off now. "I may not be going back to Wyoming. I'm considering staying on in Pine Valley, maybe for good."

"What?" Bailey's mouth dropped open. "But why? Because Abel's here?"

For a second he considered letting her think that. It wasn't the whole truth, but it would be so much easier. Smarter, too, probably.

But then he shook his head and looked her in the eye. This might be stupid. It most likely was. But he wasn't going to start this out with a lie. "No. Because you are."

Bailey stared. "Dan..."

He couldn't hold the words back. They rushed out of him like the waters of a stream after a heavy rain. "I want another shot with you, Bailey. I know I don't deserve one, and I know you've got plenty of reasons not to give me one. But I'm going to be up-front with you. You're still my wife, for the next two weeks, anyhow, and I still—" he stopped short of using the word *love*, as that would scare her off faster than anything else "—care about you. And I'd like to use that time to prove to you that I've changed. If you'll give me an honest opportunity to do that, then if you tell me no, I'll believe you. I'll sign those papers, and we can both get on with our lives."

"There's no way you could change my mind about us, Dan." Bailey sounded sure. "You'd just be wasting your time."

"Well, it's my time to waste. Just think it over, Bailey. That's all I'm asking. We're both having supper at Abel's on Friday night." He set down his coffee and stood up, settling his hat back on his head. He'd better leave before he dug this hole any deeper. "Think on it until then, and we'll talk again after. In the meantime, I'd best be getting along. I'll be back around sunrise tomorrow to work on the fence. I should be able to get the rest of the posts in tomorrow so I can start running the wire. Then I'll see what I can do about the house repairs, if that's all right by you."

Bailey stood, too. She looked alarmed, and she didn't seem to know what to say. He laid a gentle hand on her arm and felt her tense at his touch. He was making her uneasy.

"I'd just like one fair shot at changing your mind before we make our goodbyes permanent. I know our marriage isn't...real, exactly. But we did say vows to each other, and I think we should be sure before we sign those papers. Don't you?"

She didn't answer. She just looked at him, her brown eyes wide.

She sure made a pretty picture, standing there in the middle of this simple room. If things were different, if she was really and truly his wife, this home would belong to the both of them. And their babies. Surely they'd have had children—sons, maybe—with his muscles and her eyes. Or little girls who'd smile up at him and tilt their heads like their mother did.

Something broke loose in his heart and rose up to clog his throat. He needed to get out of here. "I'll see you on Friday," he managed. He headed for the door.

"I'm not going to change my mind, Dan." Bailey spoke quietly behind him.

He hesitated with his hand resting on the old brass doorknob. Then he opened the door and walked out without arguing. He'd said what he needed to say, and most likely he'd blown it. Just like he'd figured.

Outside he flipped up his collar and shivered as he headed across the dark yard to his truck. Winter in Georgia had more of a bite than he'd remembered. Right now the chill seemed to be settling right down into his bones.

On Friday evening Bailey gloomily considered the welcoming lights of Abel and Emily's farmhouse through the smudged windshield of her truck. She loved the Whitlock family dearly, and Emily's cooking was always a treat. But given her seesawing emotions about Dan, Bailey wasn't looking forward to this supper. Or to the talk Dan likely wanted to have afterward.

She'd been replaying their last conversation over and over again, seeing Dan's face as he looked at her and asked her to think about giving him another chance.

She'd thought about it, all right. In fact, she hadn't been able to think about anything else. And the more she thought about it, the more conflicted she became. Right now her heart seemed to be split right down the middle.

That was going to make it awfully hard to do the smart thing and tell him *no* tonight. But that's exactly what she was going to do. The whole point of this reunion was to bring their impulsive marriage to a long-overdue end so she could move on with her life. It was a good plan and a sensible one. And she was sticking to it.

But it wasn't going to be easy.

Dan was already here. His truck was parked by the barn. And there was a silver sedan close to the house that gave Bailey another reason to want to turn tail and run.

Lois Gordon was here, too.

Bailey didn't dislike Lois. As the doting grandmother of Emily Whitlock's older twins, Lois could be a very pleasant woman. And the elderly widow had suffered more than her share of tragedy, losing her only son, the twins' father, when he was barely out of his teens. But she was also the biggest gossip in Pine Valley, and that was saying something. She had an inconvenient talent for ferreting out people's secrets.

Bailey sighed and opened her truck door. Leaning over, she retrieved the basket of jams and jellies she'd packed up back at the store. Well, she was here now. She'd just have to watch what she said and hope for the best.

Glory, Goosefeather Farm's resident goose, watched her from the yard. When Bailey shut the truck door, the bird cocked her head and honked loudly.

"Oh, hush up," Bailey scolded.

"I haven't said anything yet."

Bailey jumped, and the jars in her basket clattered together as she fumbled to keep her grip on the gift. Dan emerged from the darkened barn.

"You scared the life out of me! What are you doing hanging around out here?"

"Same thing you were doing sitting in that truck. Stalling." As he drew closer, she caught the usual whiff of cedar, mingled now with hay. The butterflies that seemed to be ever present in her stomach these days woke up and flexed their wings. "I'm not exactly looking forward to seeing Lois Gordon again. She's hated me ever since I picked roses off her prize bush back when we were in high school."

Bailey was grateful for the dimness of the twilight. She could feel her cheeks heating up. "That was a long time ago. She's probably forgotten all about it by now, but I'm sure she'll find something else to fuss about. Come on. I guess we'd better go in."

Lois might have forgotten about those roses, but Bailey hadn't. Dan had picked them for her, and the fragrant pink blossoms had been the first flowers a boy had ever given her. For years she'd kept one dried, papery bloom pressed between the pages of her Bible.

"Before we do—" Dan reached out and caught her arm gently. "Have you thought any more about what I asked you?"

Bailey swallowed. "Please let's not talk about this right now." She glanced at the farmhouse. "If Lois overheard us, our secret would be all over town before breakfast tomorrow."

"Maybe that wouldn't be such a bad thing." When Bailey made a disbelieving noise, Dan went on. "Sorry. It's just that I'm getting pretty uncomfortable keeping all this a secret from Abel. No," he went on, when she started to protest. "I won't say anything tonight, so don't worry. I'll wait until we figure out what we're going to do. But after that, either way, I'm going to want to my brother to know the truth. Abel's been really kind, welcoming me back like he has. I don't deserve it, and I don't take it lightly. If you decide…if we end up going through with the divorce, I'll ask him to keep all this to himself, of course, but you know Abel."

Bailey did know Abel. The man had a heart of gold—and a real gift for sticking his foot in his mouth.

Abel always meant well, but if he knew their secret, he was likely to blurt it out at the worst possible time.

On the other hand, Bailey knew it wasn't fair for her to ask Dan to be less than honest with his brother.

"I'm sorry," Dan added. "I don't mean to make any more trouble for you."

She shook her head. "If I'd been honest years ago, none of this would even be an issue now. I'm the one who's sorry. When I asked you not to tell Abel, I didn't really think about the unfair position I was putting you in."

"Whoa." Dan reached out and curved a finger under her chin, tilting her face up toward his. "This is on me, Bailey. All of it. I don't want you blaming yourself. I just never expected Abel to take me back in like he has. If he'd thrown me off the farm like I expected him to this would never have been an issue. Like I said, I can wait on telling him until things are decided one way or the other. Our secret's kept this long—it can keep a little while longer."

"Thanks." She darted a grateful glance up at him. As their gazes caught, she saw his expression shift from concern into something else. Suddenly the air between them seemed oddly charged. He leaned toward her, and the barnyard around them blurred and softened.

"You're both here! Wonderful! Come on in!" Emily called from the back porch. "Supper's almost ready!"

Bailey felt as if she'd been dunked in cold water—and just in time, too. Giving Dan a flustered smile, she pulled away. Then she scurried up the steps and into the warm safety of the Whitlocks' kitchen.

"Oh, goodie! Some of your jams! Thanks, Bailey!"

Emily hurried back to her stove, which was covered with gleaming pots. Her cheeks were flushed, and her hair straggled down the back of her neck, but the table was set with a pretty checkered cloth and the air smelled delicious. "I've just got to get these biscuits out of the oven, and we'll be good to go."

"Anything I can do to help?" Dan hesitated in the kitchen doorway. Bailey kept her eyes on the bubbling food, but she could feel his gaze on her.

"Why don't you go get Abel? He's in the living room playing a board game with Paul and Phoebe. Luke and Lily are over at Natalie Stone's for the evening, bless her sweet heart. I don't know how I'd have managed with two toddlers underfoot today."

Dan vanished, and Bailey stepped over to her friend's side and began peeking under pot lids. A scrumptious-looking stew bubbled in the biggest pot, and cinnamon apples steamed in another.

"This all looks great, Emily. Need me to taste test anything for you?"

Emily laughed wearily. "If you really want to help, you could go upstairs and fetch Nana Lois. She wanted to lie down for a few minutes before dinner. Phoebe and Paul spent the afternoon with her, and as much as she adores them, I think they wore her out."

"Sure." Bailey agreed readily, but she mounted the stairs with a sinking heart. As she stepped into the upstairs hall, Lois cracked opened the door of the spare bedroom, not a silver hair out of place.

Nap, my foot, thought Bailey.

"Bailey, dear, I'm so glad to have a moment alone with you. Is he here? Abel's brother?"

"Dan's downstairs with Abel and the kids. Emily says dinner is just about—"

Before she could finish her sentence, Lois reached out and drew Bailey inside the spare room, closing the heavy door behind them.

"With Paul and Phoebe? Oh my." The older woman clucked her tongue. "That's what I was afraid of. Such a bad influence! Can you believe he's turned back up after all this time? Just like a bad penny, that's what!"

Bailey frowned. "Dan's changed a lot since he's been away, Miss Lois. And I know it means the world to Abel to have him back home."

"Dear Abel has such a trusting heart. And naturally he'd like to believe the best about his family. But, Abel, I told him, when a man like Daniel Whitlock shows back up out of the blue, you know he's up to something!" Lois shook her head sadly. "I don't think Abel can bring himself to see that." She shot Bailey a sharp glance. "I do hope *you* will be more careful this time, my dear."

"Careful about what?"

"Well, I don't mean to bring up a sensitive subject, but that young man did manage to turn your head years ago. Most unsuitable, of course, and so distressing for your dear mother, rest her soul."

Bailey felt a surge of annoyance. All right. That was enough of *that*. She should put an end to this little conversation before she lost her grip on her temper. "We'd better go downstairs now, Miss Lois. Dinner is ready."

The other woman wasn't listening. "No good ever came of associating with a Whitlock. Everybody in town knows that. Abel is the one and only exception. As for Daniel? Well, once a troublemaker, always a troublemaker. That's what I told Emily, not that she thanked me for pointing it out."

"Nana Lois? Bailey?" Emily called up from the kitchen, sounding worried. "Supper's on the table."

"We should go downstairs." Bailey pulled her arm free and opened the door.

"I'm just so concerned about dear Paul and Phoebe," Lois murmured as she followed Bailey into the hall. "Children are very easily influenced."

Bailey didn't answer. She stayed silent all the way down the stairs, devoutly relieved when they made it back into the kitchen. Lois couldn't very well keep up her fussing in front of Abel and Dan.

And that was a good thing. Bailey might have a few doubts of her own about Dan, but it still irritated her to hear Lois Gordon's pessimistic fretting. People in Pine Valley had never been willing to see the good in Dan. And there was good in him—there always had been, even back when he'd been at his lowest point. Maybe if people had spent a little more time focusing on that goodness—and a little less time spotlighting Dan's problems—things could've turned out better for everybody.

"Come with me, Nana Lois." Paul, Emily's eight-year-old son, offered his grandmother an arm. "Let me help you to your seat."

The worried creases on Lois's forehead relaxed as she beamed at her grandson. "What a gentleman you are, Paul! You take after your grandfather. He had the loveliest manners." She allowed herself to be led toward the table.

"I put Paul up to that." A basket of steaming biscuits cradled against her apron, Emily paused close to Bailey and whispered into her ear. "I wanted a chance to apologize for sending you into the lion's den. I wasn't thinking. Lois has had a bee in her bonnet all day about Danny being back home. She's part of our family, and we love her dearly, but she isn't always the easiest person to reason with when she gets on one of her rampages. I imagine she gave you an earful. I'm so sorry."

Bailey managed a smile. "Don't worry. I can hold my own with Lois Gordon. Now, something smells wonderful, and I'm starving! Let's eat."

"Sit here next to me, Miss Bailey! Please?" Phoebe, Paul's twin sister, patted the chair beside her own.

"Sure!" As Bailey settled into her seat, she glanced up to see Dan looking uneasily at the only empty chair left at the crowded table. It was right next to Lois. Dan looked as if he'd rather sit next to a rattlesnake.

He wasn't the only one less than thrilled. As he sat, Lois made a show of picking up her black suitcase of a purse and stowing it carefully on the opposite side of her own chair.

"You're the guest of honor tonight, Danny." Abel beamed from his position at the head of the table. "How about you say grace?"

"Humph." Lois's skeptical murmur was barely audible, but Bailey saw a muscle flicker in Dan's cheek. He'd heard her, as no doubt he'd been meant to.

Bailey's heartbeat sped back up indignantly, and she bit down on her tongue. Okay, so Dan didn't have the most squeaky-clean past. But Lois Gordon had plenty of her own faults, just like everybody else.

As they clasped hands and bowed their heads, Bailey heard Dan clear his throat.

"Thank You, Lord, for this food and this family and

these…friends." Bailey felt a little tickle run up her spine. Had that slight hesitation had been because of her or because of Lois? "Bless this food to our body's use and us to Your service. In Jesus's name, amen."

Bailey lifted her head in time to see Lois snatch her fingers away from Dan's. She picked up her spoon and stirred the stew in her bowl.

"My late husband was sought after for his lovely table blessings. I've always believed you can tell a real Christian by the grace he offers at a table."

"Have a biscuit, Nana Lois." Emily sounded desperate as she poked the basket in Lois's direction. "Have two."

Lois accepted the basket, but it was going to take more than biscuits to slow her down. "So, Daniel, it's my understanding that you're involved in some sort of farming enterprise out west? If that's so, I'm surprised you were able to get away for such an—extended time."

"Danny manages a ranch, Nana Lois," Abel explained proudly. "But now the rancher's grandson's taken over, so Danny isn't as needed. I'm doing my best to talk him into coming back to Georgia permanently. He says he's thinking it over."

Bailey stiffened. She glanced at Dan, and their eyes met.

"Permanently?" Lois sounded alarmed. "Are you seriously considering that, Daniel?"

"I haven't made my mind up yet. Could you pass the butter, please, Paul? These biscuits are really good, Emily."

"Of course they're good. She bakes professionally." Lois spoke impatiently. "Well, if you're considering moving here, I'd think you'd be behaving yourself a bit better. You've barely been in town any time, and you've already tried to pass a bad check to Myron Banks. You needn't all gasp at me like that! This is a small town, and word gets around. In the future you'd do well to remember that, Daniel. You won't be getting away with any of your dishonest shenanigans around here!"

Bailey saw Dan shoot a concerned glance at his brother. "The check was good. Myron just didn't want to take it because…" He trailed off. "I took it to the bank, and they cashed it with no trouble."

Bailey frowned at Lois, but the older woman was buttering her biscuit with a self-righteous expression. Bailey set her own biscuit back down on the plate. She'd lost her appetite.

It wasn't right for Dan to have to defend himself when he'd done nothing wrong. It wasn't right, and it felt all too familiar.

Caution was one thing. Caution was sensible. This was just…mean.

"You don't have to explain anything to me, Dan." Abel's lean cheeks had gone ruddy with frustration. "I can guess the truth of it. But I reckon it's a blessing you did have to go to the bank. If you hadn't, you wouldn't have been around to help Bailey when that delivery guy got fresh with her."

"Abel—" Dan and Bailey spoke at the same time, but it was too late. Lois straightened up and peered at Abel, the biscuit in her hand unbitten.

"I hadn't heard a thing about that." She sounded a little insulted. "What happened?"

Well, at least it was a distraction. "There's not much to tell," Bailey interjected quickly. "Dan stepped in before things got out of hand."

"So you see? It was a good thing he had to go to the bank after all," Abel pointed out triumphantly.

Lois's eyes narrowed. "But *why* was he hanging around Bailey's store at all? That's my question. The bank's a good little walk from there."

"Dan's doing some repairs at my new farm. For free. Isn't that kind of him?" The explanation didn't help much. Lois arched her eyebrows.

"Why would he do that? For that matter, why's he come back to town at all? I'm sorry, but somebody has to speak up here! Nobody understands the importance of family better than I do, but every family has its black sheep. Of course," Lois amended, "in the case of the Whitlocks, it's more like they had one white sheep. And that's you, Abel, dear. Daniel here has never been anything but trouble. And he wouldn't have come back to Pine Valley if he didn't want something, I promise you that. Money, most likely. I was talking about that very thing upstairs just now with Bailey."

Dan glanced at Bailey, and then back down at his plate. A muscle jumped in his jaw, and the expression on his face made her feel sick to her stomach. Her lips moved, but she couldn't seem to get any words out.

Abruptly, Dan pushed back his chair and stood. "Maybe I'd better go."

"Danny, please don't—"

Emily's protest was interrupted by the trill of Dan's cell phone. He fished it out of his pocket, looking relieved.

"It's the ranch. Colt wouldn't be calling me without a good reason, so I'll need to call him back. I'll head on back to the cabin. Abel, Emily, I'm sorry. I…" He seemed not to know what to say next. Finally, he just nodded, snagged his hat from the counter and started toward the door.

Bailey looked desperately around the table. She hated seeing that grim, defeated look on Dan's face, and she was partly responsible for it. He couldn't tell people the truth about why he was really back in town because she'd asked him not to.

Dan had his hand on the doorknob. Abel rose and exchanged a horrified glance with his wife. Neither of them seemed to know what to do.

Lois's wrinkled cheeks were a defiant pink. "Good riddance is what I say. Whatever trouble this scoundrel has come back here to cause we can certainly do well without."

That did it. Bailey stood. "Dan didn't come back here to cause trouble. He came back because I called him."

Everybody froze. Dan turned to look at her, the door open, one boot already on the back porch.

"Bailey," he said. Just the one quiet word, but she knew what he was telling her. *You don't have to do this. I can take care of myself.*

"*You* called him?" Emily looked up at Abel. "Did you know—?"

He shook his head. "No. Danny never said why he came back, and I never asked."

"You *called* him?" Lois shook her head. "Bailey Quinn! Why on earth would you do a foolish thing like that?"

"Because—" Bailey locked eyes with Dan and raised her chin a defiant notch. "He's my husband."

Chapter Seven

Three hours later, Dan stood in front of the fireplace in the cabin watching Bailey pace. She muttered to herself as she stalked from one end of the small room to the other.

"Why did I *do* that?"

Dan didn't try to answer her. Right now Bailey wasn't looking for answers from anybody other than herself.

It had taken them two full hours to pull themselves away from the chaos at Goosefeather Farm, and they were both still a little shell-shocked. There had been long explanations and apologies to work through, and he had a feeling they'd only gotten started.

He was relieved Bailey had agreed to come to the cabin, even if all she'd done so far was try to wear a hole in Abel's braided rug. He wasn't being much help, but at least she wasn't working through all this on her own.

Bailey stopped at one end of the room, staring out the darkened window, the first time she'd been still in half an hour.

Maybe it was time for him to step in.

"Bailey? Come on. Why don't we sit down and talk this over?"

She glanced at him, and his heart stuttered. Her face was so pale that her eyes looked even darker than usual.

"I've made a huge mess, haven't I?" she murmured.

Dan crossed the room and took her gently by the elbow. She allowed herself to be led to the sofa, and as Dan settled himself next to her, he prayed he'd have the ability to say the right thing.

"Look, Bailey, you have nothing to feel bad about. All you did was tell the truth, okay? And I'm glad you did."

"You can't be serious." She swallowed. "I know you were planning to tell Abel eventually, but spilling it out like that with no warning was a terrible thing for me to do. Did you see their faces? Emily and Abel were just…floored, especially Abel. I never really thought before about he'd feel, finding out I'd kept this from him all these years."

"He just needs a little time. He'll get past it. You know he will. And I don't know Emily all that well yet, but I'm thinking she's cut from the same cloth."

"Maybe, but Lois Gordon is a different story." Bailey groaned and dropped her head in her hand. "I can't believe I blurted this out in front of her. There's no putting the cat back in the bag now. It'll be all over town tomorrow. If it isn't already. Why did I *do* that?"

"You were sticking up for me." He was trying to keep a lid on his own feelings, but a crazy hope expanded in his chest as he pointed that out. "Thanks for that, by the way."

"Save it, because I don't think I did you any favors.

Please help make our
"Fast Five" Reader Survey
a success!

Dear Reader,

Since you are a lover of our books, your opinions are important to us... and so is your time.

That's why we made sure your **"FAST FIVE" READER SURVEY** can be completed in just a few minutes. Your answers to the five questions will help us remain at the forefront of women's fiction.

And, as a thank-you for participating, we'd like to send you up to **4 FREE BOOKS** and **FREE THANK-YOU GIFTS!**

Try **Love Inspired® Romance Larger-Print** books featuring Christian characters facing modern-day challenges.

Try **Love Inspired® Suspense Larger-Print** novels featuring Christian characters facing challenges to their faith... and lives.

Or TRY BOTH!

Enjoy your gifts with our appreciation,

Pam Powers

To get up to
4 FREE BOOKS & THANK-YOU GIFTS:

✷ Quickly complete the "Fast Five" Reader Survey
and return the insert.

"FAST FIVE" READER SURVEY

1	Do you sometimes read a book a second or third time?	○ Yes ○ No
2	Do you often choose reading over other forms of entertainment such as television?	○ Yes ○ No
3	When you were a child, did someone regularly read aloud to you?	○ Yes ○ No
4	Do you sometimes take a book with you when you travel outside the home?	○ Yes ○ No
5	In addition to books, do you regularly read newspapers and magazines?	○ Yes ○ No

YES! Please send me my Free Rewards, consisting of **2 Free Books from each series I select** and **Free Mystery Gifts**. I understand that I am under no obligation to buy anything, as explained on the back of this card.

❑ **Love Inspired® Romance Larger-Print** (122/322 IDL GNSN)
❑ **Love Inspired® Suspense Larger-Print** (107/307 IDL GNSN)
❑ **Try Both** (122/322 & 107/307 IDL GNSY)

FIRST NAME	LAST NAME

ADDRESS

APT.#	CITY

STATE/PROV. ZIP/POSTAL CODE

After Lois gets through spinning this, you're not going to come out looking very good. And neither am I." Bailey groaned. "That woman knows everybody in town, and I gave her the exclusive on a nugget of gossip beyond her wildest dreams. I just made her whole year, I'll tell you that." She stared distractedly at the small fire he'd kindled. "And I ruined mine."

Bailey's knee was jiggling up and down, and she was twisting her fingers together nervously. Impulsively he reached out and captured her hands. "I'm sorry. I know it's embarrassing to you, having everybody know you're married to somebody like me. I can't do much about that, but—"

Her hands, which had gone limp in his, suddenly clenched his fingers in a grip so tight that he winced. "Wait a minute. Dan, do you think I kept our marriage secret all this time because I was ashamed of you?"

Well, sure. He had thought that. Kind of. "I'm not saying I blame you."

Her eyes narrowed. "You'd better not be saying that, because it's not true! I was never ashamed to be married to you. I was humiliated that you dumped me, sure. Any bride who gets jilted before the ink on the marriage certificate is dry is going to feel pretty embarrassed. And it was even worse for me. I'd stood up for you to my parents and to everybody else in town. I believed in you, Dan, and then you dropped me after one fight. I felt like such a fool. When I finally got back home, I was too humiliated to admit what had happened, so I just…didn't."

There was something in Bailey's expression as she spoke, something vulnerable and sad that made his breath hitch in his chest. He felt an overwhelming urge to punch the man who'd put that pain on her face.

Which was a little unfortunate, given the circumstances.

"I'm sorry," he muttered raggedly. "I'm so sorry, Bailey. I honestly never thought about that side of it."

Bailey laughed shortly. "Right."

"I didn't. You were so beautiful. So smart and funny, and so special. Everybody said you were way out of my league, and down deep I knew it was true. I knew you'd be upset that I left the way I did. But later on, after your parents got the marriage annulled and you'd had time to think things over, I figured you'd be relieved."

There was a short silence, punctuated by the quiet crackling of the fire. Dan was very aware of Bailey's slim, strong hands resting in his. He should probably let them go, but he didn't want to. So far she wasn't pulling away, so he stayed still.

"I loved you back then, Dan, with all my heart. I had to deal with a lot of feelings after you left me, but I promise you, I never once felt relieved."

Dan's heart had expanded to the point that he could barely take a breath. She'd loved him. *Back then.* He felt both the joy and the sadness of that all the way to the toes of his boots. "Bailey," he said gruffly.

Something of what he was feeling must have come out in his voice, because she gently slipped her fingers free from his and scooted a few inches away. When she spoke, she kept her eyes fixed on the fire.

"Maybe it would have been easier for me if I'd understood why we even had that argument in the first place. All I wanted was for us to come back here and face up to my parents as a married couple. I didn't agree with them about you, Dan. But I still loved them, and I was their only child. I needed them in my life. I was *eighteen*, Dan."

"I know." He swallowed.

"But you wouldn't listen to reason. You told me we were going out west, period, and we were never coming back. When I argued with you, you yelled at me and stormed out."

He remembered.

"I'm sorry. I was scared, Bailey. I was sure if we came back to Pine Valley your parents would manage to break us apart. They'd been trying the whole time we'd been dating, and I knew they'd never forgive me for talking you into eloping. I was terrified they'd talk to you, and you'd wise up and realize what a mistake you'd made. Then I'd lose you for good."

She studied him for a minute. "You should have told me that."

"No man worth his salt wants his brand new wife to know he's a coward, Bailey. Maybe I should have told you. But the truth is, even if I had, I don't know that it could have worked out any better for us, not back then. You loved your parents, so you needed to come back. But my situation was totally different. If I hadn't gotten away from this place, I probably would've turned into the man everybody around here expected me to be. I needed the fresh start. But now—"

"Now you've turned that fresh start into a whole new life out in Wyoming. And I've sunk my roots even deeper into Pine Valley." Bailey shook her head slowly. "Nothing's different, Dan."

"*I'm* different, Bailey. You want to stay here in Pine

Valley? Then I'll stay here with you. Forever, if you want me to."

He saw the hope dawning in her expression, and his heart sped up. But there was doubt there, too. He held her eyes with his, willing her to believe him.

Yes, Bailey. I'm dead serious.

She pulled her gaze away, and he saw her throat pulse as she swallowed.

"What about the ranch? Your phone's been buzzing ever since we left Goosefeather Farm. You love that place, and you have friends there who obviously need you."

"Colt likes to run things by me, that's all. He doesn't really need me. And how I feel about the ranch is nothing compared to how I feel about you. If you tell me I have a chance with you, any chance at all, I'll call him this minute and put in my notice." He paused, his heart lodged so tightly in his throat he could barely breathe. "Are you going to give me that chance, Bailey?"

"Dan, I honestly don't know…"

"I'm not asking you for any promises, Bailey. Not yet. But I'm making you one. If you tell me I have any hope of winning you back, I'll put Wyoming in my rearview mirror for good. You have my word on it." He waited, watching her face. "So do I make that call or not?"

She chewed on her lip. Finally, she sucked in a quick, broken breath and nodded. "Make the call."

The breath he'd been holding whooshed out of his lungs in a huge sigh of relief. He wanted to kiss her, hug her, pick her up and spin her around.

But he also didn't want to spook her into changing

her mind, so he just took his phone out of his pocket and tapped the screen.

He'd missed half a dozen calls from the ranch. Colt probably had some new scheme about buying into the Shadow Lady bloodline he was so excited about. Well, whatever it was, he was going to have to pull it off without Dan.

Leaving Bailey sitting on the sofa, Dan started for the bedroom. Colt might not need him, but his boss wasn't going to let him go without an explanation, and he didn't want Bailey to hear that. He'd made it to the doorway when he heard the line connect. He hurried to speak before Colt could. "Hey, Colt. Listen, man. I've got something to—"

It wasn't Colt.

Dan stopped short, listening to the frantic ranch hand on the other end of the line. "I'm on my way," he said finally.

He turned. Bailey was watching him from the couch. "Dan? What's wrong?"

"There's been an accident. Colt…my boss…my friend…he's in the hospital. They don't know if he's going to make it." The awful words sounded like they were coming from someplace far away. "His wife is hurt bad, too. I have to go back to the ranch right now. Tonight."

"I see."

"I'm sorry, Bailey. I just told you I'd stay…and now…"

"It's all right." She stood up and crossed the room. And for the first time in years, she put her arms around him and hugged him tight.

The embrace was brief, but somehow it cut through the swirling confusion in his brain and steadied him.

She stepped back and looked up at him. "Now go. No," she added when he started to speak, "please don't worry about me. You go help your friends."

"I don't know how long this is going to take, but once it's over with, I'll be back. And this time I'm coming back to stay." She nodded so quickly that if he hadn't been looking for it, he'd have missed the flicker of doubt in her eyes. "You have my word on that, Bailey."

She didn't answer. She only nodded again and pressed her lips together into a sad attempt at a smile. "Take care of yourself, Danny" was all she said.

Danny. She hadn't called him by his old nickname since he'd come back, not once. It had been *Dan.*

And that's when he knew.

For Bailey, history was repeating itself. He was leaving her behind, and she wasn't sure she'd ever see him again.

And no matter how many promises he made right now, nothing was going to make her believe any different.

Three weeks later, as she drove home from the store after work, Bailey listened to Jillian Marshall's voice coming over the Bluetooth speaker she'd mounted on the dash of her truck.

"What are you going to do, Bailey?"

Bailey lifted one hand from the steering wheel and massaged her throbbing temples. The headache was no surprise. Neither was Jillian's question. Ever since she'd outed her marriage at that dinner, her life had been nothing but one big pain.

The backlash of that little bombshell, coupled with

Dan's abrupt departure, had caused a gossip storm of hurricane proportions. Her store had been mobbed on a daily basis, but nobody really wanted to buy anything. They just wanted to hear all the juicy details firsthand.

They also wanted to express their opinions. Bailey had bitten her tongue so often it was sore. And as much as she liked Jillian, she suspected that this phone call was just more of the same. Jillian was more interested in getting the scoop on what was going on than she was about the status of Bailey's foster parent plans.

Well, she couldn't really blame Jillian—or anybody else. Bailey had lived in a small town her whole life, and she knew how folks reacted to things like this. Naturally people were going to be curious.

It was her own fault for blurting out her long-kept secret like she had. She should have remembered—impulsive decisions didn't usually work out all that well for her.

Especially not when they involved Dan Whitlock.

"Bailey?" Jillian's voice came over the speaker. "Do you really believe he'll come back? I mean, I know he's supposedly dealing with some emergency, but if he hasn't even called you…"

Supposedly. Lois Gordon had done her work well. Apart from Abel's staunch belief that Danny would be back as soon as he could, that was the common theme Bailey kept hearing. Dan Whitlock had proved once again that he couldn't be trusted.

And poor Bailey Quinn had been taken in for a second time.

Unfortunately, she didn't have a whole lot of evidence to contradict either of those things. It wasn't the first time she'd found herself clinging too long to promises Dan had made.

Well, there was no point beating around the bush. Jillian was right. Dan hadn't been in touch since the day he'd left town, and that really left only one reasonable option. "The lawyer finished with the divorce paperwork last week. It just needs our signatures. If I don't hear from him by tomorrow, I'll forward it to Wyoming. Hopefully he'll sign, and that'll be the end of it."

"And if he doesn't?"

"According to the lawyer, there are some other options. But we have to try this one first."

"I'm sorry, Bailey. But don't you think this is for the best, really?"

She didn't want to talk about this anymore. "I've got to go, Jillian. I'll be back in touch once I've got the divorce papers signed, and we'll get the foster care process started."

She disconnected the call with a firm tap. She'd had enough of nosy people for one day. Now she was going to go back to her tiny little farm, love on Lucy Ball and get her animals all settled in for the night. She'd brew herself a nice cup of chamomile tea and spend the evening cuddled up with some seed catalogs.

Maybe she'd even pull out that informational packet she'd picked up at the foster care seminar. She'd take another look at those cute faces and try to rekindle the dream she'd been all too willing to set aside the minute Dan had looked into her eyes and asked her for a second chance.

If he'd really meant all those things he'd said, why

hadn't he called? At first, she'd assumed he was busy seeing about his friends. He'd call when he could. But now that Dan's silence had stretched into weeks, that excuse had worn thin.

She wasn't going to make the same mistake she'd made last time. She was older and wiser now, and she knew better. She was going to accept the reality of her situation and deal with it. Tomorrow she'd sign the divorce papers and overnight them to Wyoming. And she'd close out the Dan Whitlock chapter of her life once and for all.

"Better late than never," she said aloud as she turned into her driveway.

And then she saw his truck.

Her heart pounded as she parked, her eyes fixed on the figure slumped over the steering wheel. Dan's truck was still running, and he seemed to be asleep, his forehead resting on his hands. For once the cowboy hat was nowhere in evidence.

She walked slowly across the yard, battling her emotions at every step. Relief, joy, aggravation.

Hurt.

Well, he'd come back, just like he'd promised. But why on earth hadn't he called in all this time?

She was close enough to touch the door handle before he lifted his head. And when he did, she drew in a quick, hard breath.

The raw pain in his face made all the doubts she'd been fighting fall to the side. She yanked open the truck door and put one hand on his shoulder.

"Dan, what is it? What's happened?"

At the sound of her voice, a thin wail came from

the back of the cab, joined almost immediately by a second one. Stunned, Bailey tiptoed and saw two rear-facing infant car seats installed in the back seat. One had a pink blanket trailing out of it, the other a blue one. Both blankets were wiggling.

She turned her astonished gaze back to Dan, her heart melting at the anguish in his eyes. *"Dan?"*

It took him a minute to answer her. When he did, his voice was hoarse and broken. "The accident was bad, Bailey. They're gone. Both of them. First Angie. Then Colt."

"Oh no." She tightened her grip on his shoulder. "Oh, Dan. I'm so sorry. Are these…are these their babies?"

He nodded slowly. He drew in a ragged breath and covered her hand with one of his. "Yeah. Their twins. Finn and Josie McAllister."

"But I don't understand. Why…why did you bring them here?"

"I had to. They're mine now, Bailey. Colt wrote it all down in his will. I don't know why. Well, I mean, he left a letter. The lawyer showed me. It said I was like a…a brother to him. Closest thing to family he had. And he knew I'd take care of the twins, make sure they grew up understanding what it meant to be McAllisters. He never thought this would really happen, you know? He and Angie were young and healthy. He just needed a name, I guess. So he put mine down. He left me everything, Bailey. The ranch. All of it."

He pulled his hand away from hers and covered his eyes. It took her a minute to realize what was going on.

Dan Whitlock had always taken life's blows with a set jaw and an uptilted chin. He wasn't the kind of man who cried. He never had been, not even as a gangly teen, not even when his dad had beaten the daylights out of him.

But he was crying now.

Chapter Eight

Dan sat on Bailey's sofa, holding Josie, who was sound asleep. Bailey was sitting cross-legged on the floor, sorting through the suitcases of baby supplies he'd hauled in. She had Finn in her arms, so she sorted one-handed as the exhausted baby slept against her.

The babies ought to be worn out, the both of them. He sure was. The twins had cried off and on through most of the long drive. He'd stopped frequently, done everything he could think of to make them comfortable, but they'd still seemed miserable. He'd hated the feeling of helplessness that had given him, and he'd had to fight the urge to press the gas pedal all the way to the floor in order to get back here faster.

For the last couple of weeks, it had been all he could think about. Getting back to Bailey.

"You did a good job, Dan." Bailey surveyed the huge array of formula cans, baby medicines, diapers and bottles spread across her living room floor. "I think you have everything here they could possibly need."

"Angie's friends packed it up for me," Dan admitted. "Angie didn't have any family to speak of. It was something she and Colt had in common. But she had some really good friends."

"So did Colt," Bailey spoke softly. "You must have been an awfully good friend to him, Dan. I don't think there's a higher compliment one man could pay another one than to trust him with something as precious as these two."

The knife that had been resting in Dan's heart shifted deeper, and pain that had just started to scab over broke through again. "Like I said before, he didn't know anything like this really was going to happen, Bailey."

"But he knew that if it did, he wanted you to take care of what he loved best in the world. That says a lot, Dan. In fact, that says everything." She looked down at the tiny boy sleeping in her arms, and her face softened. "What a mercy that the babies weren't hurt in the accident."

"They weren't in the car." Dan swallowed hard. "Angie and Colt hadn't been out anywhere just the two of them since the twins came along, and it was their anniversary. So they left the babies with Angie's best friend, Mallory, so they could go out to dinner. Mallory took care of the twins for me while I was at the hospital. And later, while I was dealing with the funerals. It was nice of her because she has a two-year-old of her own to look after. She tried to teach me how to take care of them, too." He still remembered Mallory's worried, tearstained face as she showed him how to change a diaper, how to burp a wiggling baby midbottle.

She'd been as nice and helpful as she could possibly be, but Dan had seen the alarm in her eyes when he'd told her he'd be taking the twins to Georgia for a while. Not that he blamed her. The only thing he knew about babies was that he really didn't know anything about babies.

That reminded him. He fished in his shirt pocket and brought out a folded sheet of notebook paper. "She wrote down for me what to do, when to feed them. How much, and all that. I've been trying to do what she said." *Exactly* what she said, measuring formula powder out three times before he was satisfied he had it right, checking the temperature of the special sterilized water he'd bought so carefully that more than once he'd had to reheat it.

The twins hadn't been too happy about that. *Don't make hungry babies wait for food.* That was one of the first things he'd learned the hard way.

It hadn't been the last, and he was barely getting started.

"Let me see." Bailey reached for the paper, and he surrendered it with a feeling of guilty relief. She scanned the handwritten instructions quickly, her dark brows furrowed. "Okay. Nothing here looks too complicated. Just the usual baby stuff. We can manage this."

We. Dan had to fight the urge to reach over and hug Bailey fiercely with his free arm. Ever since he'd found out he was the sole guardian named for the twins in Colt's will, he'd been reeling. Finding himself entrusted with the Bar M would have been tough enough. He'd been the ranch foreman, sure, but he'd never been solely responsible for all the top-level decisions.

He'd come close, though, when Gordon's health had failed him. Dan knew most of the ropes there, and what he didn't know he could figure out. Yeah, he could manage the ranch, although taking sole charge of Gordon McAllister's beloved spread was a heavy responsibility.

But the babies? Being entrusted with the twins took everything to a whole different level. He was in way over his head, and Bailey's quiet assumption that she was in this with him, that they were going to figure it out together?

That brought such a tidal wave of relief over him that if he hadn't already been sitting down, he'd have fallen to his knees.

But he wasn't sure exactly what that *we* meant, and he was afraid to ask. His heart already felt like it had been chewed up by a wolf. He really didn't think he could handle any more pain right now.

But if it was coming, he might as well meet it head-on. "Bailey? We kind of left things hanging between us before. I guess we need to figure out where we stand now, you and me."

Bailey looked up from the can of formula she was examining, her expression wary. "Yes, I guess we do." She set the can on the floor and struggled to her feet, still holding Finn. She retrieved a large brown envelope from a table and handed it to him before sitting back down. "The lawyer finished the divorce papers."

His heart fell hard. "Is that what you want?"

She didn't answer him at first. She looked down at the infant cradled in her arms, then back at him. "I haven't signed them yet," she said quietly. "But I was planning to. I was going to send them to Wyoming. When you didn't call for so long, I figured that was what *you* wanted."

"I'm sorry about that. I just…things were happening so fast. The hospital wouldn't let me use the cell phone in intensive care, and then my battery died. I'd forgotten the charger at the cabin, and it took me a couple days to buy a new one. By that time, I was just surviving, trying to figure stuff out. And I couldn't see any way I could explain all this—" he gestured at the jumble of baby stuff all over Bailey's living room "—when I didn't even understand it myself. I figured it would be better for us to talk about it in person."

He was telling her the truth, just not all of it. Partly he'd been scared to call. He'd been afraid when she heard about the ranch, heard about how his situation had shifted, she'd back away, and he'd lose her. He hadn't been able to stand the thought of that. So he'd set his mind on getting back here as fast as he could, hoping he'd have a better chance of convincing her if they talked face-to-face.

"It's okay. I understand how hectic things get when you're in the middle of a crisis." She wasn't telling him the whole truth, either. He could see the hurt in her eyes, hear it in her voice. His silence for the past three weeks had done some serious damage.

He wanted to kick himself.

"I should have called. I'm sorry, Bailey."

"It's all right, Dan." One corner of her mouth tipped up in a smile. "At least you came back this time. That counts for a lot."

He drew in a slow breath. "I did. But I've brought along a good many responsibilities that I didn't have when we talked before."

Bailey's gaze drifted back to the slumbering baby in her arms. "You sure have. And they're beautiful, Dan. Just beautiful."

True, but the twins were only part of what he'd been talking about—and honestly, not the part that worried him, at least not where Bailey was concerned. He'd known Bailey wouldn't blink about taking on a pair of orphaned twins. She was that kind of woman—the best kind, strong and sure and good.

But the rest of it was going to be a much tougher sell, and before he tried, he needed to make sure she understood something.

"Everything's different now except for one thing. I still care about you, Bailey. I still want to see if we can work things out." He paused. "You say you were going to sign these papers because you thought that's what I wanted. It isn't, not by a long shot. But the question is, what do you want?"

He waited for her answer with his heart hammering. She took her time giving it.

"I don't know yet." Her dark eyes reminded him of a doe's, cautious and careful. "But I think I'd like the opportunity to find out."

That was exactly the answer he'd been praying for. After three weeks of grief and worry and confusion, the relief that crashed over him felt as crazy and wonderful as a thunderstorm breaking a long summer drought. But mingled in with his joy was a splinter of doubt. There were some important things about his new situation that he needed to make very clear.

Before they went any further, he had to make sure Bailey understood exactly what she was getting herself into—and exactly what he'd be forced to ask her to give up if she decided to remain his wife.

He didn't like it. But it was what it was, and she needed to know.

"Bailey," he started, but she interrupted him firmly.

"No, Dan. Please don't press me for anything more than that right now. We both need some time to process everything that's happened, don't you think? Besides, you rushed me into marrying you the first time, and that didn't work out all that well. We're going to have to take things slowly. One step at a time. And we'll see how it goes. That's the best I can do."

He stopped short. If he kept talking right now while everything between them was so fragile, he'd likely ruin the last chance he had with this woman. If he waited a few more days, let things settle a bit, maybe the connection growing between them would be strong enough to handle the weight he had to lay on it.

Bailey wanted some time, and he needed it. But that was part of the problem. Time was the one thing he didn't have to spare. And soon—very soon—he was going to have to explain that to Bailey.

The next Sunday after the eleven o'clock service, Bailey learned an important lesson: when a couple shows up at church with a pair of unexpected twins in tow, they're going to get mobbed.

Bailey stood on the side lawn of Pine Valley Community Church, surrounded by women who were exclaiming over the twins and asking all kinds of questions. She didn't mind. For the past few weeks, she'd been fielding questions about her marriage. This was a welcome change.

Besides, who could blame them? The babies were adorable, even if she did say so herself. She'd insisted on coming over to Dan's cabin early this morning and helping him get them ready for church. She knew Dan could've handled it alone. He was so careful and gentle with the twins that Bailey's heart melted every time she watched him tending to them. But she'd wanted the fun of dressing the babies herself.

And it had been pure joy. She'd loved every second of the process, even when Josie had spit up all over her pretty pink dress. Bailey hadn't minded a bit—there was a precious yellow dress she'd almost chosen, and this gave her an excuse to pull it back out. Josie looked every bit as beautiful in it, and Finn looked equally sweet in his little green romper. Bailey had taken so many pictures with her phone that they'd arrived five minutes late.

Bailey usually fretted over running late, but today she didn't care a bit. It was a beautiful, perfect Sabbath day. Spring had decided to visit Georgia early. The late-February day was unusually balmy, and the pear tree in the churchyard had already budded out in multitudes of white blossoms. The slim sapling looked like a bride, all decked out in a frothy white dress, waiting for her groom.

That image gave Bailey's insides an exciting little stir. She looked through the crowd of women to where Dan was standing in the big arched doorway of the church, talking with Pastor Stone and Abel. Jacob Stone and Dan's brother were nice-looking men, but Bailey privately thought Dan put them both to shame today. He was dressed in khaki slacks and a crisp green shirt that strained a little across his muscled shoulders. It was the first time she'd seen him in anything other than jeans, and she had to say, the man sure cleaned up well.

As if he felt her glance, he turned his head in her

direction. He didn't smile. Smiles hadn't come easily for Dan just lately. But the sun creases in the corners of his eyes deepened slightly as their gazes caught. Bailey's heart flipped over, and she had to force herself to focus her attention on the cooing women around her.

"They're so precious." Emily had Josie nestled under her chin, the skirt of the yellow dress fluffed out over her supporting arm. "Of course, you know how partial I am to twins," she added with a chuckle. "And a good thing, too, since I don't seem to be able to have anything else!" Then she sighed. "It just breaks my heart, though. About their parents, I mean."

"I know." Bailey bounced Finn, who'd begun to squirm in a way that meant he was about to start fussing. "The accident was a horrible tragedy."

She kissed the top of Finn's fuzzy head. The McAllister twins had stolen Bailey's heart from the first moment she laid eyes on them, and the attachment was only growing deeper. If things worked out with Dan, Bailey would instantly have the family she'd dreamed about for years.

But the joyful hope budding in her heart brought some guilt along with it. The twins would never have come to Georgia if it hadn't been for that terrible accident. She'd never met the McAllisters, but from everything Dan said, they'd been wonderful people.

"Yes, it *was* a tragedy." Natalie Stone reached out a finger and touched the frill of lace on Josie's tiny sock. "But our God specializes in bringing great good out of even the worst situations." The pastor's gentle wife smoothed the fabric of her simple dress over a baby bump that was just beginning to show and smiled. "I know that firsthand. I think that's what we need to focus on now—our confidence in the blessings the Lord will bring about for these little ones. I expect you're going to be a big part of that, Bailey."

"I hope so." Bailey threw a grateful look at her friend, who was living proof of God's goodness in tough situations. As a brand-new Christian, Natalie had been jilted at the altar by her irresponsible fiancé— and she'd been eight months pregnant with her son, Ethan, at the time. But God had turned that disaster into a blessing beyond imagining, and now Natalie was happily married to Pastor Jacob Stone.

Natalie's quiet words helped. Bailey felt the lingering guilt ebbing away. She couldn't change the past. But maybe, just maybe, like Natalie had said, she could be a joyful part of the twins' future.

Alongside Dan.

She drew in a deep breath of air scented with the sweetness of spring blossoms and baby shampoo and felt tears pricking at the back of her eyes. She blinked hard and smiled brightly. "Isn't this weather amazing? You'd never know it's February."

"It *is* February, though." Arlene Marvin, the church's elderly secretary, edged her way through the crowd. "No matter what that foolish pear tree happens to think. Winter's not done with us yet, and those blossoms are going to get frost nipped, you mark my words. And Cora Larkey told me to tell you those blueberries you're so fond of are blooming out, too, more's the pity."

Bailey frowned. "So early?" She loved the heritage blueberries that grew on Lark Hill Farm. They were always a huge hit at the store, and she had contracts to provide them to several area restaurants, as well.

"Yes. Our next frost'll get them for sure, but like this silly tree, they couldn't resist a false spring."

"You never know. Maybe spring's truly come early this year, Arlene," Bailey said. She realized she didn't much care either way. Blueberries and pear blossoms were small losses compared to the sweet hopes that had started to nestle in her heart.

"I doubt that. We're bound to get one more hard freeze before warm weather sets in for good. We always do. Now, Natalie, you need to get out of this sunshine and go sit down. You've been on your feet long enough. You know what Doc Peterson said."

"All right, Arlene. I'm going." Natalie gave Bailey and Finn a hug. "I'm praying for you and Dan and these sweet, sweet babies," she murmured. "Every single day."

Lois Gordon, who'd been lingering on the outskirts of the group, snorted. "Somebody'd better be praying," she grumbled. When the other women shot warning looks in her direction, Lois squared her shoulders. "Stop glaring at me. Nearly everybody in town's thinking it. Somebody might as well say it to her face. We're worried about you, Bailey. You're a good person, and we all care about you. But Daniel Whitlock is a cat of a different stripe. I know that's probably not what you want to hear right now, but it's the truth. And if you can't speak the truth in the churchyard, where can you?"

Emily lifted her chin, a sure sign that she was gearing up for battle. "I'd say if you can't show a little Christian mercy and forgiveness in a churchyard, where can you?"

Lois tightened her lips, and tears glimmered in the

older woman's eyes. "I'm sorry, Emily. I know he's Abel's brother, but they're nothing alike, never have been. Daniel took after their skunk of a father. You and Abel mean the world to me, but I'm worried about having a bad influence like Daniel around my grand-children."

"Dan had his issues in the past, but people can change, Mrs. Lois. Dan's wonderful with the twins, and he's been nothing but honest and kind to all of us since he's been back in town." Bailey spoke firmly, pitching her voice so that everybody nearby could hear. Lois was right about one thing. She was only saying what a lot of people were thinking. Bailey had heard plenty of those opinions while Dan had been gone.

It was really frustrating and very unfair to Dan. Given what he was going through right now, the last thing he needed was more of this kind of thing.

Bailey was getting pretty sick of it herself.

"I suppose people do change sometimes, but it's very risky to stake your future on it lasting for very long. Time will tell, that's what. In the meantime, the less time he spends around my grandchildren, the happier I'll be. And I certainly wouldn't rush to toss out those divorce papers if I were you, Bailey, no matter how cute these little babies are."

"Don't you worry about Bailey," Anna Bradley said firmly. "She's not rushing into anything. She's far too smart for that. She'll take her time and make the wisest possible choice."

A murmur of agreement came from many of the women. But not all of them. Bailey couldn't help noticing the worried looks some of the ladies shared.

She straightened her shoulders. So what? She couldn't

blame them for having the same doubts she'd struggled with herself.

Although ever since Dan had come back with the twins, those doubts seemed to be getting scarcer. It wasn't hard to see why. There was something so endearing about watching Dan push his own grief aside as he tried to learn how to take care of the orphaned babies. Like yesterday at the cabin, when she'd caught him scrubbing at his wet eyes with one shoulder while he struggled to dress Finn in a Daddy's Little Rancher onesie.

She'd come alongside and showed him how to roll up the tiny outfit before pulling it over the squirming baby's head. Standing so close to him, seeing the soft warmth in his eyes as he thanked her for helping...well. She wasn't quite ready yet to name what she'd felt at that moment, but one thing was for sure.

It hadn't been doubt.

"Hello, ladies." A deep voice spoke suddenly, and she looked up to see that Dan was edging gently through the women. "Hi, Emily." He nodded at his sister-in-law, who offered him a warm smile over Josie's head.

Everybody wasn't as welcoming. An uneasy silence fell, and several of the women backed away from the group and began to make embarrassed goodbye noises.

Dan's friendly expression faded into a determined politeness. "I'm sorry. I didn't mean to interrupt. I was just wondering if you were ready to go, Bailey. The twins will be kicking up a fuss to eat soon."

"Yes, I'm ready." She couldn't tell if Dan had overheard any of the women's remarks, but from that look

on his face, it didn't matter. He'd clearly picked up on
the guilty glances the women were tossing around.

Bailey's heart sank. So far Dan had quietly accepted
everything this town had thrown at him, but Pine Valley's lingering suspicions had to bother him. He'd come
back to his hometown grieving and trying his very best
to parent two orphaned babies, but people were still
giving him sideways glances.

He deserved so much better. From all of them.

Dan had come up in front of her and was reaching
for Finn. Before she thought better of it, Bailey went
up on her tiptoes.

And for the first time in well over a decade, her lips
met Dan Whitlock's.

She heard the swift intakes of breath around her,
but the women weren't the only ones caught by surprise. She felt Dan startle, for just a second. Then the
arms that had been reaching for the restless baby went
around her waist instead and pulled her into the warmth
of his kiss.

The feel of his lips on hers was at once sweetly familiar and unsettlingly new. Her heart hammered fu-
riously as emotions she'd kept dammed up for years
broke free and washed over her like a waterfall.

It was all over in a few sweet seconds, but that didn't
matter. Bailey felt the impact of Dan's kiss all the way
to the tips of her toes. When she went back down on
her heels, she had to brace her knees to keep them
from buckling.

Maybe she should have thought this through a little better. Unfortunately, right now her brain couldn't
have come up with a rational thought if her life had
depended on it. She was barely able to stay upright.

Dan must have seen something in her face, because he quickly scooped the warm bundle of baby out of her arms. Then he cupped her elbow with one hand, steadying her.

Her heart hammering with a frantic mixture of joy and daring, Bailey looked up into his face. His greenish-brown eyes locked onto hers, but instead of the joy she'd expected, she saw shock mingled with something else, something that made uneasy goose bumps pop up on her arms.

When Dan finally spoke, his words came out in a guilty rush. "Bailey, I think we need to talk."

Chapter Nine

When Bailey's face changed, Dan knew he'd messed up.

As they walked toward his truck, each of them holding a squirming twin, he cut worried sidelong glances at her. She kept her eyes away from his, her jaw clenched. She didn't speak, but he didn't need her to. It was plain enough to see that he'd embarrassed her—and probably made her mad to boot.

He hadn't meant to. That kiss had just thrown him for a loop, coming out of nowhere like it had. He felt like kicking himself. He'd been hoping and praying for something like this for so long—and when it had finally come, he'd blown it.

What he'd said was true. They did need to talk. But he shouldn't have blurted that out in front of all those ladies. Apparently, Abel wasn't the only Whitlock with a talent for sticking his foot in his mouth.

When they pulled out of the church parking lot, he glanced at Bailey. "I thought we'd go to the cabin. We can feed the twins and put them down for their naps. And then we can talk."

"All right." That was all she said, but he saw the

tense furrows deepen on her forehead. Bailey already suspected she wasn't going to like what he had to tell her.

He didn't like it, either. Gordon McAllister hadn't only shown him the ropes of ranch work—the old man had also given him some no-nonsense lessons about honor. One of the main things the rancher had stressed was the fact that a decent man never went back on his word.

But that's just what Dan was about to do.

They pulled up into the cabin driveway and began the process of getting the twins out of their car seats and into the house. They worked together to warm up tiny bottles of formula, change diapers and settle the sleepy twins into the cribs Dan had arranged against the wall of his bedroom.

For the first time since he'd become responsible for the babies, he wished they'd take some extra time to settle down. He needed some time to think through what he was going to say. But once their bellies were full, the little traitors dozed off. Both of them. At the same time. That almost never happened.

Go figure.

Dan glanced at Bailey, who was tucking a giraffe-printed blanket around Finn. Her face was relaxed and unguarded as she hovered over the sleeping infant, and Dan's heart tightened in his chest. He really didn't want to have this conversation right now. He wanted more time, but that sweet, unexpected kiss had forced his hand.

If he wanted more of those kisses—and he definitely did—he had to be completely honest with Bailey. There was no way around it.

"They're down," he whispered. "Let's go." He backed up against the full-size bed to allow her to pass by him. He noticed she pressed herself tightly against the crib rails in order to squeeze by without brushing against him.

So they were back to that.

Once in the living room, Dan paused to pull the bedroom door closed. Bailey frowned.

"Shouldn't we leave it open so we'll hear them if they wake up?"

Dan laughed wryly. "Don't worry. In this little cabin, you'll hear every squeak. Trust me on that."

Bailey nibbled on her lower lip as she sank down on the sofa. "Maybe we should alternate nights, so I can help out more. I could stay here with the twins every other night, and you could bunk out at my place. You're having to miss a lot of sleep trying to take care of them all by yourself."

That was kind of her, but it wasn't what he was shooting for. He wanted all four of them together in one house, living like a real family. But at least her offer gave him a flicker of hope that he hadn't messed things up too badly.

Not yet, at least.

He sat beside her, leaving a careful gap between them. "I appreciate that, Bailey, but until you and I work things out, the twins are my responsibility. Don't get me wrong, I'm really thankful for all your help, but I'll handle the night shifts solo for now. I still don't have a clue what I'm doing, but I don't think I'm messing up too bad."

Some of the color returned to Bailey's face. "You're not giving yourself enough credit. You're wonderful with the twins, Dan." Her expression softened. "You're going to be a great dad."

She sounded like she truly believed that. His eyes met hers, and his breath got caught someplace midway between his chest and his throat. Suddenly all he wanted in the world was to take this woman in his arms and kiss her again.

He'd better get this over with before he lost what little self-control he had left.

He cleared his throat. "Like I said back at the church, Bailey, we need to talk."

"Because I kissed you." Bailey was watching him closely. "I'm sorry, Dan."

"Don't be." The words burst out of him. "I'm not a bit sorry you kissed me, Bailey."

"Okay." A shadow of a smile drifted across her lips as she studied him. "I'm glad to hear it. But I shouldn't have surprised you like that, right there in front of everybody."

He drew in a long slow breath. He shouldn't ask her. He should go right ahead with what he needed to say.

But he couldn't help it. He had to know. "Why, Bailey?"

"You're actually going to make me spell it out?" Bailey made a rueful face, but she nodded. "Okay." She tilted her head and looked at him steadily. "I've been asking God to help me build a family, and I thought I knew how He was going to do that. But now I'm wondering if maybe He has a different idea. I don't have everything figured out yet, Dan. But I think, maybe, I'd like to see if you and I can make this marriage work."

And there it was. Everything he wanted, there for

him to take, like a rosy ripe apple hanging temptingly on the lowest branch of a tree.

As she waited for him to answer, her lips were trembling just the tiniest bit, so slightly that most folks wouldn't even have noticed. But he noticed everything about Bailey, and he knew that she'd just put her heart out on the line for him. Again.

And he knew what that was costing her.

It was costing him, too. Costing him everything he had not to take her into his arms, kiss her senseless and tell her she'd just made him the happiest man on the planet. Not too long ago, that's exactly what he would have done.

Now he couldn't—not until he made sure Bailey understood exactly what she was getting herself into. But first he had one last question of his own.

"Please don't take this the wrong way, but I have to ask you. Is this…" He trailed off. This was hard. "Is this just because of the twins?"

Or does it have anything to do with me? With us? He left that part unsaid, but it hung in the air between them all the same.

"No." She paused. "At least, not entirely. I won't lie to you. I'm so in love with those sweet babies already that I can hardly stand to be away from them. But I also care about you, Dan. Or I'm beginning to. Watching you navigate your way through this crisis, as bad and tragic as it's been…well, it's been beautiful. You've been so faithful, so determined to take care of the twins, even though I know you're way out of your comfort zone. It's changing the way I see you, how I feel about you. It's as simple as that."

She was *so in love* with the twins, but she *cared*

about him. He wished those two expressions had been reversed. But still, given their past, even those words coming from Bailey felt like seeing spring flowers poke their heads through the dirty mush of leftover winter snow.

But she was wrong about the *simple* part. Nothing about this was simple.

"I'm not saying we should rush into anything," Bailey went on. "That's what got us into trouble the last time. This time we should take things nice and slow. We have a lot of details to work out. You'll need to find a job, and we'll need to get the house fixed up. By that time, people around here will have realized how much you've changed, and all this silly gossip will have died down. And maybe, when we're ready, we can have a little vows-renewal ceremony. Nothing fancy. Just something to mark our fresh start in front of our friends and neighbors, you know? If Finn and Josie are going to grow up here, I think it might be important to do that. Don't you?"

He had to tell her. Now.

"Bailey, if you want a ceremony, I'm all for it. We'll do whatever you want to do. But Finn and Josie won't be growing up in Pine Valley. I'm sorry, but I have to take them back to Wyoming."

"What?" She couldn't believe what she was hearing. "But I thought that part was already settled. If I... if we decided to try to work things out, you were staying here. You gave me your word, Dan."

"I know what I said." His face had gone pale. "And at the time I meant it. I'm sorrier to break that promise to you than I've ever been about anything, Bailey. But please understand, my whole life has changed since then. Colt didn't just trust me with the twins, he trusted me with the Bar M, too. I can't let him down."

But you can let me down. "I see."

"I hope—I hope with all my heart—that you do see. Because I said my whole life had changed, but really that's not true. One thing hasn't. I still want you to be my wife, Bailey. I want us to make a life together, be a family together, you and me and the twins. And just now you told me it's what you want, too. That's what really matters, isn't it? Where we live is just geography."

"So where we live doesn't matter, but we have to live in Wyoming? That's the decision you've made for both of us. Without even discussing it with me first." She couldn't keep the bitterness out of her voice—not that she tried all that hard. "This is starting to feel really familiar, Dan."

There was a short, pained silence before he answered her. "But I'm not making a decision, Bailey. Not this time. I'm just stating a fact. As the owner of the Bar M, I have to live in Wyoming."

"Why? Couldn't you sell it?"

Shock tightened his face, followed by a swift, definite shake of his head. "You don't understand how things are. We're talking about a family legacy. That ranch is the twins' birthright. Generations of McAllisters have poured their blood, sweat and tears into the Bar M. It's not something I'd feel right about selling."

"Maybe that's true, but the problem is I own a business, Dan. Here, in Georgia. And I just bought a farm. I've got a mortgage to pay. I can't just dump all that and follow you out to Wyoming. It would mean giving up everything I've built, everything I've worked for."

Dan nodded slowly, his eyes intent on hers. "I understand. You've got a lot on the line here, and you have every right to be upset. I know it's a big thing to ask. But I think you'd love Wyoming, Bailey. It's beautiful there—a different kind of beautiful than here, that's true. And living on a ranch can be hard sometimes, but you've never been afraid of tackling tough things." One corner of his mouth tilted up slightly. "You took me on."

"I did. And I'm not really sure bringing that up helps your argument." She shook her head. "I don't know, Dan. I just don't see any way we could make this work."

"I know this is coming out of nowhere, Bailey. But you said a minute ago that you thought you saw God's hand in this. Right? And you and I both know that sometimes the Lord chooses to take us down roads we'd never have picked out on our own. Maybe this is one of those times. Would you at least pray about this before you make a decision? Please?"

She didn't answer him right away. Her emotions were swooping around like the swallows she'd had to evict from her farmhouse's old chimney.

One thing was for sure. History really did repeat itself, just like people said.

If you let it.

A muffled whimper came from the bedroom. Bailey stood, grateful for the interruption. "That sounds like Josie. I couldn't get her to burp after her bottle, so she's probably got a tummy ache. I'd better go get her before she wakes Finn up, too."

Dan had risen, too, and he put a gentle hand on her arm. "Bailey. Please."

"I'll pray about it, Dan." It wasn't so much a promise as a statement of fact. Of course she'd pray about this. What else could she do? This was too big to handle without God's help. But no matter what choice He led her to, one thing was for sure.

She was going to end up losing something important.

"Thanks, Bailey." Dan spoke with a quiet gratitude as he followed her toward the bedroom, where Josie's whimper was escalating into a full-fledged fuss. Before Bailey made it to the doorway, a second angry wail started. They hadn't been quick enough, and Finn was joining forces with his cranky sister.

So much for naptime, but Bailey didn't blame the babies a bit.

Right now, she felt like crying, too.

Chapter Ten

"So? What are you going to do?" Trisha Saunders leaned over the counter at Bailey's, her beady eyes alight with excitement.

Bailey gritted her teeth behind a bright smile as she finished ringing up the local florist's half pound of dried apricots. She'd never cared much for Trisha. "I haven't made a decision yet."

That was at least the twentieth time she'd said those words this morning. Trisha's reaction was the same as everyone else's.

"Oh?" Trisha looked disappointed. She'd obviously hoped to leave Bailey's with some juicy gossip to add to her apricots. "Really? Well, if you ask me, I wouldn't consider it for a minute. No sense throwing your life away for a man like Dan Whitlock."

"Nobody's asked you that I heard. And who says she'd be throwing anything away?" Arlene Marvin was next in line, holding a packet of loose-leaf herbal tea that Bailey knew perfectly well the caffeine-addicted church secretary would never drink. Trisha wasn't the only one here under false pretenses this morning.

Being caught in the middle of a gossip storm might be good for business, but that was the only silver lining Bailey saw in it. She was so sick of this—she wanted to go home, lock the door and hide.

But she couldn't do that. She had a store to run whether she felt like it or not.

"Your receipt is in the bag. Have a great day!" *And don't let the door hit you on the way out.* Bailey held out the apricots, but Trisha was too busy glaring at Arlene to notice.

"Of course that's what she'd be doing, Arlene! Giving up a successful business and moving all the way to the middle of nowhere to raise somebody else's kids? For a man who's already dumped her once?" Trisha shook her head. "I don't see how any woman with half a brain could do a thing like that."

Arlene snorted. "I don't see how any woman with half a heart could do anything else. Those poor, orphaned babies need a mother. What's a grocery store compared to that?"

Bailey gave up and set Trisha's bag on the counter. "Excuse me." She attempted to reach past Trisha to get to Arlene's tea. Neither woman glanced in her direction.

"You don't know what you're talking about, Arlene. You're from a different generation, and you haven't built a business from the ground up like Bailey and I have. No matter how much she cares about the twins, Bailey has to look after herself. She needs to be sensible."

"Well, I may not know much about running a business, but I do know there's nothing sensible about love," Arlene announced solemnly. "And I don't be-

lieve for a minute that those twins are the only ones
Bailey cares about. Bailey kissed Dan Whitlock in the
churchyard right in front of God and everybody. She
wouldn't have done that if she didn't trust him, and if
she trusts him, maybe we should, too!"

Bailey felt her cheeks flushing as she finally managed to snag the packet of tea from Arlene's gesturing
hand. How could these women talk about her personal
life as if she weren't standing right here? "Arlene, you
do realize this is decaf, right?"

"That's fine, dear," Arlene said absently, proving
once and for all in Bailey's mind that this little visit
had nothing to do with buying tea—or anything else.

"That was before all that stuff on the internet came
to light." Trisha turned to Bailey. "She didn't have all
the information then. Isn't that right, Bailey?"

Bailey had no idea what Trisha was talking about.
"What—" She stopped the question short. If she asked,
she'd be throwing fuel on this fire, and that was the last
thing she wanted to do right now. She needed to get
these ladies out her door, and not only because she had
half a dozen other customers milling around.

Dan was bringing the twins by in a few minutes
so that he could spend the day working on the farmhouse. She definitely didn't want him walking into the
middle of this.

"That will be five dollars and thirty-five cents, Arlene," Bailey said.

"Pooh!" Arlene said dismissively. She was rummaging around in her large black purse, and for a second
Bailey thought she was fussing about the price of the
tea. "You shouldn't pay attention to the nonsense people post on the internet, Trisha. You'd be better off

paying attention to what the pastor has to say about gossip."

"*You're* fussing at *me* about gossiping, Arlene Marvin? Maybe you should pay attention to Pastor Stone yourself! You're the biggest gossip in this whole town!"

Arlene's face flushed a mottled magenta, and Bailey winced. This was rapidly getting out of hand, and her other customers were beginning to take notice.

"Ladies, please," she began, but the women ignored her and continued to speak over each other, punctuating their fuss with plenty of *I never*s and *of all the nerve*s.

Bailey felt a reassuring squeeze on her forearm. Natalie Stone had slipped beside her.

The pastor's wife cleared her throat. "Arlene?" No response. The other two women were intensely focused on each other, and their discussion had grown so loud it was starting to echo. Natalie tried again. *"Arlene!"*

Arlene turned her eyes to Natalie and blinked. Natalie smiled her gentle smile, but Bailey saw a glint of steel in it. "Jacob is looking for you. Apparently the choir robes arrived, and they seem to be the wrong color."

"What?" Arlene's eyebrows, which were already at a dangerous level, rose up into her hairline. "Wait a minute. Are they maroon? Don't even answer me. I'm sure they are. That Mavis Jones! The committee made it perfectly clear that the robes were to be a lovely pale blue, but she was dead set on that horrible maroon. Kept saying we'd all change our minds if we could just see them. Not likely! The only taste Mavis has is in her mouth. You tell Jacob not to worry. I'll get those things returned for the right ones." Arlene hurried toward the door, muttering. "Maroon, my foot! If I don't give Mavis a piece of my mind."

"I think maroon is a lovely color," Trisha said irritably. "I honestly don't see how Jacob puts up with that woman, Natalie. She's so opinionated!"

Natalie made a noise that could have been a laugh, but she disguised it deftly with a cough. "Trisha, wasn't your Pekingese outside tied to the bike rack?"

"Yes. Why?" The florist squinted through the window. The bike rack was empty. "Oh no!" She ran out of the door, leaving her apricots behind on the counter, calling her dog.

Bailey watched her go with a feeling of relief. "Well, I hope she finds her dog safe and sound, but I also hope it takes her a while."

"I imagine it will. Her husband was the one who untied him, so they're probably at home by now." Natalie blinked innocently. "Maybe I should have mentioned that, but she ran out of here so fast I didn't have a chance."

"Thanks," Bailey shook her head admiringly. "You pulled that off like a champ. I owe you one."

Natalie chuckled. "No, you don't. I'm a minister's wife, and I know what it's like to be the star goldfish in the town's fishbowl. This will all blow over, Bailey. Just hang on until it does. And don't pay any attention to what people say. Things get so exaggerated, particularly on the internet. People will post things online they'd never say in person. Well," Natalie added with a second wink, "except for Trisha and Arlene. Those two will say pretty much anything right to your face."

There was that internet thing again. Bailey frowned. "What are people posting on—" Before she could finish, a car honked from outside. A silver sedan had pulled up to the curb.

"There's Cora. She's coming with me to my ultra-sound appointment today. She's so excited about being an honorary grandmother to this new baby, she can hardly stand it! I'd better scoot on out before she comes inside. The last thing you need is Cora weighing in on your personal business, and I know she wouldn't be able to resist." Natalie gave Bailey a quick hug. "Jacob and I are praying for you. All of you. God will work this out for the best. Just trust Him."

With one last squeeze, Natalie was gone. Just as she reached the door, Dan walked up.

He set both of the twins' carriers on the sidewalk to open the door for Natalie. She paused briefly to ex-claim over the babies before climbing in the passenger side of Cora's car.

Bailey hurried to the door and held it wide so that Dan could bring in both twins at once. "Thanks," he murmured, and a tiny smile ticked up his lips. As Bailey stared up at him, all rational thought left her brain, and her heart sped up into what she privately called "Dan gear."

One thing was for sure. She was never going to be able to make a sensible decision if this kept up.

"Where do you want me to set them down?" Dan asked.

Bailey took hold of the handle of Finn's carrier. "I cleared off some space on the table behind my counter. That way I can keep an eye on them while I'm work-ing. I've got a playpen folded up in the back. I'll bring it out when they wake up."

As they got the babies settled in the middle of the

wide wooden table, Bailey fussed over the blankets. She couldn't resist trailing a finger over Josie's plump cheek. The infant girl stirred in her sleep, poking a tiny foot out from under her blanket.

The dainty sock Dan had put on her was half-off, and Bailey gently readjusted it. "How long have they been asleep?"

"They zonked out on the ride over. I fed them right before I left, and I've got a couple of bottles already made up in their bag. We'll need to stick those in your fridge. I changed them right before I put 'em in their car seats, so they hopefully should be good for a little while." He glanced around the busy store. "Maybe they'll let you get a little work done before they wake up. Once they do, though, it's a whole different ball game. Could be this wasn't such a good idea, my bringing them over."

"Don't be silly. I'll love having them here." She smoothed Finn's blanket and glanced up at Dan. "Don't worry about them for a minute. I'll keep them the rest of the afternoon and bring them home after work."

Bailey glanced around the store. Her remaining customers were keeping a wary distance now, shooting curious glances toward them, but not venturing close. She knew that the minute Dan stepped back out the door, they'd be making a fuss over the twins and asking more nosy questions.

She wasn't in any particular hurry for that. "What are you planning to work on today?"

"I'm done with the fence, so I'll be working inside. I've noticed a couple more repairs that I'd like to get done, and I need to pick up some things from the building supply. Then I'll be heading over to your place."

"More repairs?" Bailey frowned, noting the tired lines in the corners of his eyes. "You look exhausted already. With the twins keeping you up most of the night, you sure don't need to be working yourself into the ground over at the farmhouse all day."

He drew in a slow breath. "Got to. I had a call from the ranch this morning. One of the top hands is dealing with everything for me while I'm here. He's doing his best, but he's in over his head. Looks like I'm going to have to get back even sooner than I'd thought."

Bailey's heart fell. "When?"

He paused. She saw in his eyes that he didn't really want to tell her. But he did. "Soon, Bailey. Within a week. I'm sorry. I know this is rushing you, but I don't have much choice, not if I want to keep the ranch afloat."

Bailey managed a jerky nod. "I see. Well, even more reason not to worry too much over the repairs, Dan. You can't possibly get much done in that amount of time, and there's no point wearing yourself out trying."

"I want to do as much as I can, though, Bailey. I promised I'd see to this for you."

He had. But then, he'd promised her a lot of things. "I really wish you wouldn't worry about this, Dan. You've got enough on your plate right now."

"I want to do what I can," Dan repeated stubbornly. He had his cowboy hat in his hands again, running it around and around like he did when he was uneasy. She felt a sudden urge to snatch it and fling it across the store. That out-of-place hat was a stark reminder that Dan was out of place here, too.

He waited a second or two then clapped the hat back on his head. "I'd best be getting on with it. If the twins get to be too much, just call me. And we'll…" He hesitated. "We'll talk more this evening. Okay?"

She knew what that meant. He wanted her answer about Wyoming. And she still didn't have one.

"Sure." She managed a quick smile, but her heart wasn't in it.

He nodded, his eyes searching hers. His gaze slid over to the dozing babies for a second, and his jaw tightened. Then he turned and headed for the door.

Just as she'd suspected, the instant he was out on the sidewalk, her customers flocked to the twins. Bailey smiled wearily as the handful of women exclaimed over the babies.

She made a sudden, highly unusual decision. She couldn't take much more of this, not today. Sidling past them, she went to the door and flipped the store sign to Closed.

Once she waited on these people, she'd take a break. She'd sit down for a few minutes while the twins were still asleep, do some more praying and try her best to figure out what answer she was going to give Dan.

The customers were in no particular hurry to leave, but finally only Anna Bradley was left.

The bookstore owner pushed her weekly supply of cookies across the table with a sympathetic smile. "You've got your hands full, don't you? In more ways than one. I felt bad coming in here this morning when I saw how swamped you are, but you were totally right when you suggested these cookies. If I don't keep a plate of them out by my coffeemaker, my customers will riot."

"Believe me, Anna, I don't mind seeing you, not one bit. How's the baby?"

Anna's face lit up. "He's wonderful! Oh, that reminds me." She rummaged in the cloth shopping bag swinging on her elbow and produced a book with a smiling baby on the cover. "I brought this for you. I've read just about every baby book out there, and this one is definitely my favorite. No," she added as Bailey reached for her purse, "it's a gift. Trying to keep Turn the Page up and running with a baby on my hip is a real challenge. I don't see how Emily manages twins and the coffee shop, but she does. You're so blessed to have her as your sister-in-law. She can give you lots of tips about balancing twins and a business, I'm sure."

Bailey slipped the cookies into a bag. "Well, it doesn't look like I'll be dealing with the twins *and* a business. It seems like it's either-or."

Anna nodded seriously, twining one long strand of her curly hair around her finger. "Yes, I'd heard Dan was planning to move back to the ranch. But I'd thought maybe, you know, given what people out there are saying about him on the internet, he might be reconsidering staying in Pine Valley."

There it was again. This time she was getting to the bottom of it. "Anna, what are you talking about? What's on the internet?"

Anna's eyes widened. "You don't know? Oh, Bailey. I'm sorry—I assumed you'd heard all about it. The bookstore's been buzzing with it this morning."

Bailey shook her head. "I haven't heard a word about it. What's going on?"

Anna hesitated, but when she caught Bailey's eye, she reluctantly explained. "Trisha Saunders found a newspaper website for Broken Bow, Wyoming. There was an article posted there about the twins' parents.

And there was a comment option, you know, so people from the town could express condolences or…whatever."

"And people were saying negative things? About Dan?"

Anna nodded slowly. "Some were. About half of the comments were about the McAllisters: what a wonderful couple they were, and what a tragedy the accident was. But the rest of them were all about Dan." Anna bit her lip. "But I'm not sure you can put a whole lot of stock in that, Bailey. You know how people are. They say all kinds of things that aren't strictly true. Especially online."

Bailey glanced back at the twins. Finn had his mouth open and was snoring gently, and Josie had her head cocked sideways.

They were so incredibly beautiful. She couldn't imagine giving them up.

And Dan. If she let him go back to Wyoming without her, she knew she'd likely never see him again. The very idea made her feel sick to her stomach.

She believed Dan had changed. She did. But she'd blindly followed her feelings for Dan into trouble before. She couldn't make that mistake again.

Probably Anna was right, and whatever was being posted on the internet wasn't anything worth paying attention to. But given the circumstances, Bailey needed to be sure. She was going to have to find that website and read those comments for herself.

"Anna? I hate to rush you, but I think I might head home for a little while."

"Of course, Bailey. And I hope… I really do hope things work out for the very best. For all of you."

"I do, too, Anna," Bailey said quietly. "I do, too."

* * *

At the building supply, Dan took his time flipping through the book showing windows that could be ordered. He'd already found the one he needed for Bailey's spare bedroom. That had taken him all of five minutes. Now he was just biding his time until Myron Banks finished waiting on the only other customer in the store.

Dan had taken the precaution of going by the bank and cashing a check, and his wallet was stuffed with hundreds. But he wasn't in the mood to have Myron's sorry-I-can't-take-your-check-son conversation in front of anybody else. There was enough gossip going around this town already without adding more to it.

Dan shut the window book and opened the book on doors. That back door of Bailey's needed to be replaced. He'd noticed some splits around its base, so he figured he might as well add a door to the order.

Of course, Bailey was right. There was a limit to how much he was going to be able to get done in a week, and he couldn't stay longer. In fact, given the conversation he'd had with Jimmy this morning, a week was stretching it.

Jimmy had sounded stressed. "Guy came rolling up with a trailer this morning, had three heifers on it. Said Colt paid him half up-front for 'em and was supposed to pay him the rest on delivery. It was a lot of money, Dan. I didn't see as I had much choice but to write him a check, but there ain't much left in the account now. I don't mind overseeing the cattle and the hands while you're gone, but this finance stuff is more than I feel comfortable with. You got to tie up whatever loose ends you've got hanging down there and get on back."

After promising to come back as quick as he could, Dan had sighed, closed his eyes and pressed the hot phone against his forehead. So Colt had finally found some Shadow Lady heifers somewhere—and apparently he'd paid a pretty penny for them. Jimmy wasn't kidding, either—the ranch wasn't flush with cash right now. Dan needed to get back there and get down to the business of sorting everything out.

As best he could, anyway.

The truth was, he didn't know much more about the financial side of things than Jimmy did. A little, thanks to helping out Gordon all those years, but not a lot. He was going to have plenty of learning to do—and he'd be doing it with the twins in tow.

And maybe without Bailey beside him. Her reaction this morning when he'd told her about the deadline had twisted his stomach into a leaden knot.

It was written plainly on her face. She still wasn't any too sure about the idea of relocating to Wyoming— or about trusting him with her future. He'd had to fight himself to keep from getting down on his knees and begging her to give him a chance.

Right now, the hope that he and Bailey could set things right between them was the only sliver of good that he saw left in the world. Well, that and the twins. If he could keep the babies safe and if he had Bailey by his side, then he could handle anything life threw at him. He knew that. But if he had to go back to the Bar M without her…

Please, Lord. Don't make me face that.

"You done hanging around back there, son? You may have the day to waste, but I don't."

Myron's gruff voice startled Dan out of his thoughts.

"No, sir. Truth is, I don't, either." He walked up to the rough wooden counter and pushed a handwritten slip of paper across it. "This is what I need."

Myron scooted his reading glasses down on the end of his nose and peered at the list. "Passel of stuff again." The man lifted his rheumy blue eyes and studied Dan over the half-moons of his lenses.

"How much?"

"Hold your horses," Myron grumbled, pulling his adding machine across the counter. "Gonna take me a minute. All this for Bailey Quinn's place?"

Dan didn't bother to hide his sigh. Pine Valley gossip even made it into the building supply, apparently. "Yes, sir, it is."

"That's who you was doing that fencing for, too, so I heard."

"That's so." He looked pointedly at the gnarled fingers resting idly on top of the adding machine. "You mind getting this totaled up for me? Like you said, I don't have a lot of time to spend waiting around."

"From the look of this list here, you got no choice but to do some waiting." The man glanced back down the items. "I got some of this in stock, but I'll have to order the rest."

This wasn't good news. "How long will it take to get here?"

"Delivery truck just ran yesterday, and it won't be back for a couple of weeks."

Dan's heart fell. He'd be long gone by then. He'd have to figure out a plan B. "Okay. Just get it ordered, please."

Myron nodded, and the keys of the adding machine began to chitter. Dan stood there breathing in the scent

of sawdust and studying the calendar tacked crook-
edly on the wall behind Myron. It was a month behind.

Dan wished the calendar was right. A month ago,
things had been so different. A month ago, he could
have kept his promises to Bailey, and the twins would
have been safe and happy with Colt and Angie.

Now it seemed like the whole world had been
flipped upside down, shaken hard and handed to Dan
to fix. He didn't know what he was going to do, but
he knew he couldn't afford to mess up. And he sure
couldn't afford to put his personal hopes and dreams
ahead of what he knew was right.

No matter how desperately he wanted to.

When Myron finally announced a total, Dan lifted
an eyebrow. "That's lower than I thought it would be.
You sure you added it right?"

The old man shot him a hard look. "I been doing this
since before you were born, so don't you go questioning my work. The total's right. I gave you a discount.
It's a big order, and it's for Bailey." Myron jutted out
his chin. "I'm right fond of that little lady. She always
gets a discount here."

In spite of everything, Dan felt his mouth twitching
upward. "She's worth being fond of."

"Ain't she, though? Spunky, too. Don't take nothing from nobody and can outwork a man most any day.
Not that outworking a man's much to brag about these
days. Men ain't what they were back in my day, that's
for sure." The old man shot him a look. "I hear you're
a pretty good worker, though."

Surprised by the compliment, Dan froze, his wallet halfway out of his jeans pocket. "Thanks," he said
finally. "I try to be."

"You planning on writing a check, are you? No, now, don't go all hotheaded on me. I was just going to say, it's fine by me if you want to. I'd have taken your check the last time if I'd known you was working for Bailey."

"As it happens, I've got the cash handy. But I appreciate it, just the same." Dan counted out the bills, and Myron began fussing with making change.

"Well, next time, you don't worry about it. Your check's fine here. Bailey Quinn wouldn't put up with any shady dealings, not from you nor from anybody else. She's a smart girl. But I reckon you know that much already. Heard you married her back when the two of you was just wet behind the ears."

"I did."

"Well, more power to you. I don't care a bit what those old women say with their wagging tongues. I don't blame you. A man finds a woman like Bailey Quinn, of course he's going to marry up with her if he can. Parting company with her, that's a horse of a different color. That there seems mighty stupid to me."

"I won't argue with you."

"But then I don't imagine you'll be making that same mistake again. Will you?"

"I don't want to." Dan accepted his change. "But some of that's up to Bailey."

Myron nodded. "If I were a younger man, maybe I'd have given you a run for your money. But as it is, I'll just give you a little advice. First off, you hang on to Bailey if you can, and don't you hurt her or you'll be answering to me." The other man thumped his bony chest with one finger.

Dan kept his lips straight. "I hear you. Anything else?"

"Yeah. Don't you pay any mind to all the stuff

they're saying on those internets. Nobody in their right mind pays any attention to that kind of nonsense." Myron scrawled out a receipt. "I'll get everything I got in stock delivered in an hour or so."

"That'll work." Dan folded up his receipt, puzzled. What did Myron mean about the internet?

"That all you needed, son?" Myron asked. Suddenly there was something so fatherly about the old man that Dan found himself grinning.

"For now." Dan stuck out his hand. "Thanks."

"You're welcome enough, I reckon," Myron said gruffly. His hand felt papery dry in Dan's. "You be sure to give Bailey my best, now."

"I'll do that."

Out in the parking lot, Hoyt Bradley was getting out of a hulking work truck. The building contractor caught Dan's eye and nodded. "Danny."

"Hoyt, it's good to see you." Dan stuck out a hand, wondering if Hoyt would take it.

Hoyt had been the quarterback of the football team back in high school, and Dan had been a running back who made more trouble than he was worth. Hoyt had taken plenty of heat for Dan back in the day, and they hadn't parted on the best of terms.

But Hoyt hesitated only a second before giving Dan's hand a hearty shake. "Good to see you, too."

"Listen, Hoyt, I need a word with you. You got a minute?"

"Right now? No, I'm sorry, I don't. I got my guys waiting on some stuff out at the job site." The other man hesitated a second then fished in his pocket and produced a business card. "Here. My number's on there. You can call me tonight, if you want." Hoyt waited a second before asking, "You needing some help, Danny?"

"'Fraid so. I'm in kind of a jam right now."

"Yeah. I heard about that. You ask me, people ought to be ashamed, writing stuff like that online instead of saying it straight to a man's face. Don't know what I could do to help you out with that, though." Hoyt glanced quickly at his watch. "Computers aren't really my thing. And I really do have to get back to work."

Computer stuff? Dan's mind flashed back to Myron's remark about the internet. What were they talking about? "No. This has nothing to do with…that." Whatever it was. "The help I need is more up your alley. And I'll be paying you for your time, too."

Hoyt nodded, looking relieved. "Call me, then, and we'll hash out the details tonight. See you, Danny."

Dan spent the rest of the drive to Bailey's place mulling over Myron's and Hoyt's comments, but when he parked beside Bailey's truck in the driveway, he wasn't any closer to figuring things out.

In fact, now he had another question. What was Bailey doing home at this hour? Had the twins been too much trouble for her to keep them at the store?

If so, he owed her an apology. He took the porch steps two at a time and pushed open the door. Finn and Josie were lying on a red-and-white quilt folded thickly on the floor, kicking their feet and making soft grunting noises. Bailey was on the sofa, intent on the laptop she had propped on her knees.

"Bailey?" When she heard his voice, she jumped and snapped the laptop closed. She looked up at him, her face stricken, almost guilty, and Dan suddenly felt a rush of weariness so profound that he wanted to lie down and sleep for a month.

Maybe longer.

Something fishy was going on for sure. And he honestly didn't think he could cope with any more trouble at the moment.

But as usual, he didn't have a choice.

"I guess you'd better tell me what's on the internet that has everybody around here talking, Bailey."

"Dan, I don't think—"

"I need to know."

Bailey hesitated a second. Then she reopened the laptop and tapped a few keys. She set it beside her on the couch and rose to her feet.

"Here. See for yourself. Watch Finn, won't you? I think Josie needs a diaper change." She leaned over to scoop up the baby and hurried out of the room.

Chapter Eleven

Fifteen minutes later Bailey came back down the steps, Josie cradled in her arms. As she turned to go into the living room, the baby stirred against her. Bailey nestled the tiny girl closer, settling her cheek against the infant's downy head and breathing in the sweet baby scent. A quivering thrill ran through her, fierce and unmistakable.

It might be wrong of her to feel so hopeful after reading the remarks on the webpage she'd found, but she couldn't help it. Now maybe Dan would change his mind.

Lord, please. Use all that mean-spirited sniping on the internet for good. Let it show Dan that Wyoming's not as good an option for us as Georgia. Let him decide to stay here with the twins, because I really don't think I can stand to let him go.

She kissed Josie on the top of her head and walked across the sagging floorboards into the living room. It was empty. Her laptop was resting on the sofa, closed, but Dan and Finn were nowhere to be seen.

She hurried toward the window. When she saw

Dan's truck was still in the driveway, she exhaled the nervous breath she'd been holding.

He was still here, but where was he? She was about to check the kitchen when she saw Lucy Ball trotting around the corner of the house. The calf had picked up a fallen pecan branch and was carrying it carefully in her mouth.

Dan must have let her out. That meant he and Finn were outside. Snatching up Josie's rose-colored blanket, Bailey headed out to find them.

She didn't have to look long. Dan was standing in the side yard, Finn cradled in his arms, squinting up at the farmhouse. He seemed to be deep in thought, but when Finn squeaked and flailed a tiny fist, Dan gently raised the baby up and kissed the wiggling hand.

"It's okay, buster. I've got you."

"Dan?"

He turned at the sound of her voice, and his slow smile warmed his face. It didn't quite reach his eyes, though, and she could see the tired worry there. "That calf of yours was bawling, so I let her out for a minute." Dan shook his head and chuckled softly. "You're rubbing off on me, Bailey. Now I'm treating that little Jersey like a puppy, too." He nodded back at the farmhouse wall. "You've got some rotten siding there that'll have to be replaced. Not much, but some. I ordered some at the building supply today, and Myron should be delivering it pretty soon. But I didn't think to get a ladder. You don't happen to have one lying around someplace, do you?"

"Not one that's tall enough for that." Bailey watched Dan closely. "Are you okay?"

"Me? Yeah. Finn here is a different story." Dan

glanced down at the baby in his arms. "I'm thinking he may need a diaper change. I'll take him inside and see to that before the delivery truck gets here."

He started toward the side steps leading up to the porch, but Bailey caught his shirtsleeve as he passed her. "Dan, don't you think we should to talk about it?"

"Talk about what?" He raised an eyebrow. "All that junk on the internet? Not really. It doesn't matter, Bailey."

Bailey had been braced to see Dan angry and hurt, maybe even bitter. But Dan seemed none of those things. If anything, he seemed indifferent.

Which, given how passionately he'd spoken to her about the Bar M and his friendships there, didn't make a lick of sense.

"Why didn't you tell me about it?"

He frowned. "I didn't know about it, Bailey."

She waited, but he didn't add anything else. She hated to rub salt in a wound, but he was going to have to spell this out for her. "You didn't know any of it? You didn't know people were saying you conned the McAllisters into leaving you the ranch? That you'd cheated the twins out of their inheritance?"

He was looking down at her, his eyes shaded by the brim of his hat. A tiny muscle in the corner of his mouth pulsed.

"People don't generally say things like that to a man's face." He paused. "I got a feeling something was going on when I was back in Broken Bow, but it was nothing specific. It was more of a…whiff of trouble. Kind of like Finn's diaper right now." He smiled, but there was no humor in it.

"Why didn't you mention that to me?"

"I don't know." The smile faded as he studied her. "Like I said, I didn't think it mattered that much. Does it, Bailey? Do you need me to tell you that none of the things people are saying are true?"

Something in his expression made her flush. "I don't believe you conned anybody, Dan. But are you telling me it doesn't bother you that people think you did?"

Dan shrugged. "One thing I've learned, Bailey. People are going to think what they want to think." One corner of his mouth lifted a little. "I guess when you've been on the ugly side of public opinion as often as I have, you get kind of philosophical about it. Changing people's opinions is a dicey business, and it's not something you have a whole lot of control over. I do my best, and I try not to worry too much about what folks say."

He waited a second or two, then added. "If you have questions, Bailey, you don't have to go looking stuff up online. If you want to know something, just ask me. I won't lie to you."

There it was—the first little note of hurt she'd heard in Dan's voice. And it was there because she'd gone online rather than come to him with her questions.

Fine. She'd ask him, then.

"Is it true that the ranch is bankrupt?"

"No." Dan's response came instantly. "There's no denying that we've had some tough years, and money's pretty tight. Before Gordon passed on, we'd gotten the ranch back in the black, but then Colt took over, and…" Dan trailed off and cleared his throat. "Colt was one of the best men I ever knew, but he wasn't that good with money. He had big ideas, and he hadn't spent enough time in the past couple of years actually working the ranch to know where the soft spots were. So from what I can tell, he dug himself into a hole."

"I see." Bailey felt nerves start to form a lump in her stomach. Leaving Georgia to take charge of a ranch with money problems. It sure didn't sound very…sensible.

Dan crooked a finger under her chin and lifted her face so that they were looking into each other's eyes. "It's nothing I can't fix, Bailey."

She nodded and managed a weak smile back. "Right."

"I saw Gordon build the place back up, and I know a little bit about how to go about that. I'm not saying I won't make my share of mistakes while I figure stuff out, but we're probably looking at only two or three more lean years before the ranch is turning a solid profit again."

Josie whimpered, and Bailey resettled the infant, patting her freshly diapered bottom gently.

It was so hard to think with Dan's hand under her cheek. His thumb was tracing her chin. The touch was gentle, but it was so…*there*. She couldn't afford to get distracted. She needed to see this through. "Is it true that one of the neighboring ranchers wants to buy the ranch?"

Dan removed his finger, but he held her gaze as he nodded slowly. "I haven't had an offer, but probably so. The Jensens own the spread next to us, and they'd love to get their hands on the Bar M. I wouldn't be surprised if I heard from Neal Jensen shortly." Dan blew out a short, frustrated breath. "He's a skinflint, so he'll offer me half what the place is worth and get hot when I don't take it. But he'll come around in time, and so will the rest of them. The ranchers need each other too much to stay mad for long."

"How can you be sure? Some of those remarks seemed so mean-spirited. I'm sorry, I don't mean to make this worse. I just...don't see how you can be so determined to go back to a place full of people like that."

To her astonishment, Dan gave such a belly laugh that Lucy Ball, who'd been stealthily approaching them, dropped her stick and bolted back toward the barn.

Neither of the twins was too happy with the sudden noise, either. They set up fussy protests, and Bailey and Dan spent the next few minutes shushing and soothing.

When they had the babies calmed, Bailey spoke in a whisper, "I don't get why that's so funny! It's a legitimate question."

"Bailey, maybe you don't know because you haven't ever lived anywhere but here, but every place is like that. Pine Valley is like that. Not for you, maybe. But for some of us, it is. People are people the world over. Folks are saying some mean stuff, sure. It's what people do when they're grieving. They talk out of their hurt, and they look around for somebody to be mad at. But underneath all that, most of these people are good folks. I know that about them, even if they're not so sure about me right now."

That reminded her. "What about the other thing they said. About your drinking?"

The world really didn't get any quieter after she asked that question. The babies still snuffled, and Lucy Ball loped back by chasing a gray-striped hen who'd escaped the coop and was squawking for all she was worth.

But the silence from Dan was so loud that it was all Bailey heard as she waited for his answer.

"I've been sober for over ten years. I saw that remark about me hanging out at the bars. That was wrong, or at least," he amended, "it's wrong now. I'm telling you the truth, Bailey."

She believed him, but— "You're not worried that all this stress—the twins, the ranch and all the rest of it—won't tempt you to—"

"No. I fought that battle, Bailey, and with God's help, I won it. My drinking days are behind me. So, no. I'm not worried." He waited a second or two before speaking again. "Are you?"

She started to tell him no, of course she wasn't worried. But then she stopped herself.

Because it just wasn't true. "Yeah, Dan. I'm worried. Not necessarily about you drinking, but you've got a ranch that's struggling and twins to cope with and a community that sure isn't coming across as supportive as you made them out to be. And then—" She hesitated. She didn't even like to bring this up, but— "Somebody mentioned that there was some question about the twins' guardianship."

"There isn't."

"Are you absolutely sure?" Of all the snarky comments, that one had struck the most fear in her. "Maybe we should have a lawyer here look over the papers. Do you have them with you?"

"The papers are all in order, Bailey. Both Colt and Angie were only children. They didn't have any close family to take their babies. I'm not saying they couldn't have chosen somebody else, but they definitely made the twins my responsibility. They're my son and daughter now, and I'm going to do the best I can by them." He looked down into Finn's face, and Dan's expression shifted in a way that made her heart clench tight and warm up all at the same time.

Dan Whitlock was a fine-looking man no matter what he was doing. But when he was looking down at his new son with his heart in his eyes… Well, then he was so drop-dead gorgeous that when he lifted his head and looked at her, all starch went right out of her knees.

"I really want the four of us to be a family, Bailey. I know that comes with a steep price tag for you, and I'm sorry. But there's not much I can do about it."

"Maybe there is, though, Dan." She rushed forward, desperately. "I still don't see why you couldn't stay here. There's somebody who wants to buy the ranch, and you said yourself the place is struggling. Wouldn't selling it be the most sensible thing to do?"

Dan shook his head. "We've talked about this already, Bailey. Selling the ranch isn't an option. The Bar M has been in the McAllister family for generations."

"But you're not a McAllister, Dan. And neither am I."

"Finn and Josie are. As far as I'm concerned, the Bar M is theirs, no matter what the legal papers say."

"They're only babies, Dan. They don't have any emotional attachment to the ranch. You don't even know for sure if they'll want to be ranchers when they grow up. If you sell the place, you could put the money into a trust for their educations. That way they could choose their own paths."

"I'll make sure they get whatever kind of education

they need, but I'll find a way to do it without selling their birthright. I'm sorry, Bailey, but like I've said before, I don't have a choice here. Colt knew that I'd see this the way he and his grandpa did. He trusted me to do the right thing."

"But is it more important to do the right thing for the McAllisters or for *us*, Dan? My business is turning a solid profit. You keep talking about the importance of family? Well, your family, your real family, is in Pine Valley. Abel and Emily are just a few miles down the road, and the twins could grow up knowing their cousins. Do we really want to give all that up for a ranch that could very well go belly up and leave us with nothing?"

Dan studied her, a muscle jumping in his cheek. "You really think I'd let that happen, Bailey? That I'd ever see you and these babies left with nothing? You don't believe that I'd make sure the three of you had everything you needed?"

"Dan—"

Just then a horn blew behind them. A large truck with Banks Building Supply in script on its sides was pulling into the driveway.

"The material's here." Dan looked down at Finn. "I'll go get him changed real quick. Then can you watch the twins while I help get the stuff unloaded?"

"Sure." There was something stiff about the way he asked, like he was asking a stranger for a favor. It hurt her heart. She snagged his sleeve as he passed her. "Dan, I care about you, all of you. I do."

He halted, but he kept his eyes fixed on the approaching truck. "I believe you care, Bailey. I just don't think you trust me all that much. And that's where we get mired up, you and me. Every single time."

And with that, he left her and headed into the house.

The next afternoon, Dan stepped back from the tractor and wiped his greasy hands on a rag. "Try her now, Abel."

Abel obliged by turning the key, and the tractor sputtered before choking down again. "Still not quite there."

"At least she's turning over. I'll do some more adjusting, and we'll see where we are."

"All right. But before you get back into it, there's something else I'd like you to have a look at. Wait here a minute."

Abel climbed off the tractor and disappeared out the barn door. For a few seconds, the only sounds were the contented clucking of the Goosefeather Farm hens in their enclosure and an occasional honk from Glory the goose, who was strolling around the yard. Dan finished wiping off his fingers, a waste of time since they were just going to get greasy again, and waited uneasily.

Looked like Abel was finally getting around to the real topic he'd wanted to discuss when he'd summoned Dan over here. Dan had known this wasn't really about a broken-down tractor. It had taken Abel long enough. They'd been working in the barn for the better part of two hours.

Not that Dan was complaining. Abel probably wanted to talk about all the sniping plastered across the *Broken Bow Tribune*'s website, and Dan wasn't particularly anxious to have that conversation. Focusing on the ailing tractor had been a welcome distraction.

Abel came back in with a folded-up paper in his hands. "Here," he said, thrusting at Dan. "This is for you."

Dan unfolded the paper and scanned it. It was some kind of legal document. Dan didn't speak lawyer all that fluently, so it took him a minute to figure it out. "This is the deed to the cabin."

Abel nodded. "And the ten acres around it. Emily and I have talked it over, and we're agreed. We want you to have it."

Dan shook his head and held the paper out. "I can't accept this, Abel."

Abel made no move to take it. "Sure you can."

"I guess this means you've heard about the stuff on the internet. So what, now you're going to try to talk me into living at the cabin instead of going back to Wyoming?"

"Nope. The cabin's yours free and clear. You can sell it if you want. Use the money for whatever you might need back at that ranch of yours."

"Thanks, but I don't need a handout, Abel."

"Good, because I'm not giving you one. I'm just splitting things up fair, that's all. I kept the fifteen acres that adjoin Goosefeather, and I've been think-ing ever since the twins were born that I needed to move my woodcarving shed closer to home. So this makes sense."

Dan shook his head and set the deed on the worn seat of the tractor. "You're not fooling me. You saw that comment about the ranch being underwater financially, and you're trying to help me out. I appreciate it, but there's no need, Abel. I'll have the Bar M back where it ought to be soon enough, and I'll do it on my own."

"I don't doubt it."

"Then you're the only one that doesn't." Dan reached back into the engine. This conversation had gone about far enough. "Let me tweak this a little more and we'll see how she does. I think we've just about got her straightened out."

That was Abel's cue to climb back up on the tractor, but he stayed where he was.

"You're talking about Bailey, aren't you? 'Course you are. She's the only person whose opinion you've ever cared much about apart from your own. Danny, I don't have much business giving anybody advice, but I'm going to give you some anyhow. You've got to stop pushing Bailey. If you don't, you're likely to lose her for good."

"Seems like that's going to happen anyhow." Dan weighed the wrench in his hand.

"And that's scaring you to death and making you stupid. You know better, Dan. You have to. You've worked around animals, and people aren't that different. You push 'em, they just dig in their heels and fight you harder. 'Specially if they've been hurt in the past. Trust takes its own sweet time, Danny. You can't rush it."

"Then there's no hope, I guess." Dan's heart sank to the bottom of his boots, and he flung the wrench onto a nearby hay bale. "Bailey still doesn't trust me as far as she can throw me, and I'm leaving at the end of the week."

"As long as we've got the Lord in our corner, there's always hope. Sometimes He likes to show off by waiting until the last minute, and sometimes He doesn't answer our prayers the way we want Him to. Could be Bailey's not the only one who's got to learn how to trust. Leave it in His hands, Danny, and see what happens." Abel hoisted himself back up onto the tractor. He plucked the folded deed off the seat and held it out wordlessly in Dan's direction.

Dan hesitated, then he took the deed from his brother's hand and stuffed it in his pocket. "All right. Let's get this tractor running. I guess I'd better go have a talk with Bailey."

Chapter Twelve

Bailey grabbed the lowest plank of rotten siding with both hands and gave a mighty tug. Nope. It still wasn't loose enough to come away. She looked down for the crowbar she'd dropped on the ground a few seconds ago, but it had disappeared.

"Lucy!" Bailey spotted the calf a few yards away. She'd dropped the metal tool on the ground and was nosing it curiously. "I need that!"

She'd known better than to let the calf out when she was trying to work on a project, but nowadays the house just seemed so empty whenever Dan and the twins weren't here. When a person was miserable and lonesome, even the company of a mischievous calf was better than nothing.

Bailey was determined to stop mooning around and worrying. Even if Dan did go back to Wyoming, it wasn't the end of the world. She'd had a perfectly good life all planned out here before Dan had come back, before he'd brought the twins into her life. If Dan was determined not to listen to reason, she could go back to that plan and be perfectly happy.

Eventually.

That's what she was telling herself, anyway. If it seemed a little hard to believe right now, that just meant that she had to try harder. She needed to start handling things on her own again, like she'd been doing before Dan's truck had rolled up in her driveway.

To start with, she could rip down some of this rotten siding Dan had pointed out. But she needed her crowbar.

Lucy watched Bailey's approach cautiously. "I need that, Lucy." Bailey took another step, and Lucy rolled her big brown eyes and nudged the crowbar an inch or two on the grass. "They're rotten enough to need to be replaced, but not rotten enough that they come off easy. Although," Bailey added in a mutter, "I don't know why on earth I expected anything about this house would be easy. Everything has been a challenge right from the start, and things just keep ballooning. Wyoming's starting to look not so bad."

She was joking. Sort of. Sure, homeownership was turning out to be tougher—and more expensive—than she'd expected, but so what? She'd gone through the same sort of stuff when she'd opened Bailey's, and she'd made it through that. Now the store was doing great.

Well, more or less. Not only was she coping with an endless flow of customers who really just wanted to chat about her personal life, but yesterday she'd received the official word that Lyle's grandfather was taking her off his delivery route. She'd spent most of the afternoon trying to find another organic citrus supplier, but her options didn't look good.

That plus the house problems plus the whole dilemma with Dan was pushing her stress level into the danger zone. But, she reminded herself, pretty much anything worth doing had its tough moments. That came with the territory.

She just wished all the hard stuff wasn't happening at once. It was chipping away at her resolve to stand her ground.

"You don't want to move to Wyoming, do you, Lucy Ball? Probably not. You wouldn't be the star of the show. Lots of other pretty cows out there."

Lucy Ball huffed at her and shifted her weight. Then the calf leaned down, nimbly picked up the crowbar in her mouth and dragged it farther away.

Bailey sighed. She knew the drill. Lucy Ball's interest in that crowbar would last about as long as Bailey's did. If Bailey left her alone, Lucy would probably abandon the tool in search of something else.

"It's a good thing you're so cute." Bailey shot the calf a dirty look before turning back to the house. She'd give that siding another mighty pull and see if she could get it to give way with just her hands.

She'd succeeded in loosening it a little more when she heard Dan's pickup crunching up her gravel driveway. Her heart immediately leaped up and wedged itself in her throat.

Bailey tiptoed and tried to see into the truck cab. Had he brought the twins with him? She darted a quick look at the watch on her arm. Nearly time for a bottle. She'd knock off work and feed Josie for him. The baby girl always lost interest in her bottle before Finn lost interest in his, and she was so much tinier than her brother. Bailey had discovered that if she burped Josie a little more frequently, the baby would take an ounce or two more formula.

Bailey started toward the truck, but she only made it a few steps before Dan climbed out of the cab. Alone.

"Where are the twins?" she called, not quite able to keep her disappointment out of her voice.

"I asked Emily to watch them for me for a little while so we could talk."

Bailey shivered suddenly, and she rubbed her hands up and down her arms. Three guesses what he wanted to talk about. He needed a definite answer, and she didn't have one. Whenever she tried to pray about it, she just ended up having imaginary arguments with Dan about staying in Pine Valley. If he pressed her now, she was going to have to say no. It was the only sensible thing to do. Her brain knew that. Her heart was arguing with her, the same way she'd argued passionately with her mother back when she was eighteen.

You can't throw just your future away for the sake of that Whitlock boy, Bailey! You're smarter than that!

But I love him, Mom!

Dan walked over and squinted up at the siding. "You're trying to take this off by yourself?"

"Yes, but I'm not getting very far. I can't pull it loose with just my hands, and Lucy stole the crowbar."

"Of course she did." Dan grabbed hold of the piece she'd been fighting with and pulled it free in one quick move. He tossed it on the ground.

"Show-off." She wrinkled her nose at him. "And just so you know, I loosened that up for you."

"Yeah, I noticed. I was planning to get these boards down for you, Bailey. I just got tied up over at Abel's."

Bailey shrugged. "Don't worry about it. I know you don't have much time. I can manage."

Dan sighed deeply, but he didn't argue. "Look, I'll put this board someplace Lucy can't get hold of it, and then we need to talk. Okay?"

Bailey nodded. They'd talk. But if he wanted an answer from her today, he probably wasn't going to like what she had to say.

They settled on the porch rockers. Dan looked out over the budding forsythia. "I forget how early spring sets in around here. Hard to believe it's only February, with things already blooming."

"It's nearly March. The forecast is calling for a freeze tonight, though." Bailey pointed at the fruit trees, frothing white beside the house. "Bad news for those. I was excited when I saw all the blooms, but Arlene was right. I doubt there'll be any apples or pears this year. *Early springs bring false hopes.* That's what the farmers around here say."

Dan nodded. "After a long winter, a nice warm spell is mighty welcome. But then when the cold comes back, it feels even sharper."

Bailey was watching him closely. "Sometimes it causes a lot of damage, too."

He didn't think they were talking about the weather anymore.

Dan looked down at the hat he was holding in his lap. "Bailey, listen. I know you don't understand why I'm so set on going back to Wyoming, but I want you to know that it's not because I don't care enough about you to stay. The truth is—" He halted, his heart pounding so hard he could hear its pulse against his eardrums as he struggled to find the right words to go on with. "The truth isn't just that I love you, Bailey. It's that I don't think I ever stopped loving you. In all the years we've been apart, there's never been anybody else for me. The other guys used to rag me about that some." One side of his mouth tilted up as he remembered. "Called me Brokeheart. Kept introducing me to girls. I even went out with a few. I didn't know we were still married. I thought for sure we weren't. But even so, I never asked anybody out a second time. It didn't matter how pretty they were or how sweet. They weren't you, and I couldn't get past that."

To his surprise, Bailey reached over and took his hand in her own. "If you really feel that way, then don't go, Dan. Sell the ranch and stay here with me. Let's build a new life together with the twins."

"I can't do that, Bailey. It's killing me. But I can't." He took a minute to get hold of himself before he went on. "And I can't keep asking you to give up your life to come with me, either. I did that before. I was wrong to do it then, and it's just as wrong of me to do it now. And just like last time, I've made this all about me, whether you cared about me enough, whether you believed what I said or what other people said about me. I'm sorry for that. Wyoming taught me a lot of things, Bailey. And one thing was that a man doesn't ask for anything that he hasn't earned, fair and square. I haven't had the time to earn your trust back like I'd hoped to. So I'm not asking you to trust me, not anymore."

Bailey's lips went pale, but she squeezed his hand gently. "I wish—I really wish—it could be different, Dan."

"So do I." He looked down at their entwined fingers. "It's funny. Your hand always felt like it fit so perfect in mine. It still feels that way to me. Our lives, though. They never did seem to fit together like that."

"No. I guess not."

There was just one last thing he needed to do, and he'd stalled long enough. "Wait here a minute. Okay?"

Bailey rose, watching as Dan walked to the truck. Part of her mind was noticing that there was something grim about the set of his shoulders. The other part was trying to memorize everything about him before he disappeared from her life again.

Because from what he'd just said, it sure sounded like that's what he was about to do.

She felt a flutter of panic. She wanted to call after him, tell him she'd changed her mind. That she would go with him after all.

She bit her lip and stayed silent, her pulse pounding. It was a painful place to be, caught here between her breaking heart and her hard-earned good sense. But she couldn't let that pain push her into making another mistake.

Dan fished around inside the truck cab for a minute. When he headed back toward the porch, he held a large brown envelope in his hand. Bailey knew what it was even before he handed it to her. Her heart went ice-cold.

"You signed the divorce papers?"

He nodded. "They're notarized, so everything's in order. You be sure to look them over, but I think you'll find everything you're going to need is in there. All you have to do is sign them, and it's a done deal."

Bailey looked up from the envelope. "This is what you want?"

"No." His answer was swift and sure. "It's not. But if it's what you need, I want you to have it." He looked away from her, off to the new fence standing strong and straight around her little pond. "I'm sorry, Bailey. I came back here to try to make things right between us, but all I ended up doing was making more promises to you that I couldn't keep." He darted an apologetic look back at her. "Seems I've got a habit of that where you're concerned, and I know I'm causing you even more hurt this time. You've gotten attached to the twins."

"Very." She wasn't sure about much right now, but there was no doubt about that.

Dan didn't smile, but the crinkles in the corners of his eyes deepened as he looked at her. "I don't know much about mothers. I never knew mine very well, but I'd say you've got the makings of a great one. I didn't bring the twins with me today because I figured we needed to have this one talk without any pint-size distractions. But if you want to see them again, to say goodbye, I'll bring them over before I leave town."

Bailey shook her head. *To say goodbye.* If she saw the twins again, if she had to kiss them knowing it was for the last time, she'd fall apart into a million pieces.

"No, Dan. I appreciate the offer, but I don't think I could handle that. It's not that I don't care about Finn and Josie, I want you to know that. I care too much, I guess. I hope you understand."

"Yeah, I do."

"But I'll be praying for them and for you every day." Bailey cleared her throat, trying her best to cling to the scraps of strength she had left. "You should probably get the twins' things to take with you. I've got the portable cribs, and some outfits…"

"You keep those things. You'll likely be needing them for some foster babies soon."

Bailey's stomach twisted painfully. Maybe that idea should have brought her some comfort, but it didn't. "I bought them for Finn and Josie."

"I know. I appreciate how kind you've been. But Bailey, this isn't easy for me, either. I just don't think I could stand looking at all the cute things you bought for them. Seeing those reminders every day would just keep me wishing things were different. Know what I mean?"

Bailey nodded. She knew.

But it was what it was, and the sooner they got this over with, the sooner they could both move on with their lives.

"All right. I'll keep the things. And if I don't manage to pull everything together to be a foster mom, I'll just give them to Jillian. I'm sure she can find somebody who can use them."

"You'll be able to pull things together. I'm sure of it." Dan's eyes zeroed in on hers. "But no matter what happens from here on out, remember this. You're always going to own a big chunk of my heart, Bailey. That's never going to change. If there's ever anything you need me to do for you, anything at all, you know where to find me."

"At the Bar M." She couldn't quite keep the sadness out of her voice.

"Yeah." He held out his hand for her to shake, and she took it in her own. But then she tiptoed up and kissed him on his stubble-roughened cheek, just a little southwest of his lips.

For a second she thought he would turn his head and turn it into a real kiss, but he didn't. Instead, as she drew away, he looked down into her eyes and gave her hand a gentle squeeze.

"I'll be—" He stopped. "I was going to say I'd be seeing you. But I reckon I won't be, most likely. But I'll be thinking about you, Bailey, you can count on that." One corner of his mouth tipped up. "Same as always."

He gave her hand one last squeeze, then he released it and went down the steps.

One of the saddest things in the world, Bailey thought, was watching somebody you care about drive away. But she watched until Dan's pickup had vanished behind the pines.

Then she sank back down on the rocking chair. Just a few minutes ago, the air had seemed almost balmy. Now she felt chilled.

She stared into space for a few minutes, watching Lucy Ball. The calf had finally abandoned her crowbar in favor of a bright pink watering can. Bailey had snagged it at the dollar store, and she'd absentmindedly left it in the yard after watering the daffodil bulbs she'd planted along the front of the house.

It was made of plastic, and Lucy would destroy it in no time flat. Bailey would have to figure out some way to take it away from her.

But first… Bracing herself, Bailey bent up the metal tabs securing the flap of the envelope and pulled out the sheaf of papers. Flipping through them, she saw Dan's scrawled signature everywhere it needed to be. But when she got to the end of the documents she'd given him, there seemed to be a few extra sheets tacked on. Bailey scanned then, frowning.

It took her a minute or two to absorb what she was reading, but when she understood what she was looking at, she was still confused. This didn't make any sense.

Dan had enclosed the deed to Abel's cabin, along with the paperwork necessary to transfer it into Bailey's name. There was a sticky note stuck on the last page.

> *Abel gave me the cabin free and clear. I didn't want to accept it, but you know Abel. He was too stubborn to take it back. You understand how I feel about this place, so I'm giving it to you. You're probably shaking your head right now.*

Bailey gave a surprised, tear-clogged laugh. She was, actually.

> *But don't feel bad about taking this. The time I spent at this cabin was the worst part of my life in Pine Valley. But the time I spent with you, Bailey Quinn, that was the best. I want you to sell it and use the money to make your dreams come true. God bless you. Dan*

It was a lot to take in. So Bailey sat on the porch until the afternoon faded while tears streaked down her chilly cheeks, watching Lucy Ball break the watering can into half a dozen pieces.

Chapter Thirteen

Early the following Saturday morning, Bailey stood barefoot in her kitchen having a fight with her sink.

She hadn't intended to get up this early. The ache she'd felt in her chest watching Dan drive away hadn't eased off any. Sleep was the only relief she got, but last night she'd dreamed nonstop about Dan and the twins. She'd woken up with tears on her face, and the pain had been almost unbearable. She'd finally thrown back the covers, even though it was still dark and she wasn't supposed to open the store until ten.

She'd get some coffee, spend some time praying and reading the Bible, then start making lists of all the home repairs she needed to get done for the foster care home study. Once she got that process rolling, she'd get her energy and her enthusiasm back.

Of course she would.

Unfortunately, her morning plan had hit a snag when her sink decided to be a brat. The old faucet handle was stuck and wouldn't turn. It was offering only the tiniest trickle of water, and this was interfering with the all-important production of her first cup of coffee.

This was not okay. She definitely needed coffee—probably a lot of coffee. Otherwise she didn't know how she could possibly face another long, miserable day of minding her store when all she could think about was how much she missed Dan and the twins.

She hated feeling like this. It wasn't like her. She loved her little store. She'd loved it since the day she'd held her grand opening, but now she dreaded going in every day. The idea of standing behind that counter for another eight hours made her feel sick to her stomach.

Of course her only other option was stay home, and that didn't sound any more appealing. Everywhere she looked, she saw something else that needed fixing. Once seeing the projects all around her had felt energizing. Now it just felt exhausting.

And at least at the store there was coffee.

Bailey sighed. She had to stop moping around and take charge of her life again. She'd start by dealing with this stupid faucet.

"Come *on*," Bailey muttered. She took hold of the handle and wrenched it wide-open, hoping to get a better flow.

Instead, the handle broke off in her hand. The frustrating trickle stayed exactly the same.

For a second or two, Bailey just glared at the metal and porcelain handle lying on her palm, willing herself not to fling it across the room.

"This is only temporary." She spoke aloud, her words echoing in the empty kitchen. "I'll get back to the way I used to be sooner or later, and things will be fine."

In spite of the encouraging words, Bailey found herself blinking back tears. Her new tendency to start crying at any moment was getting out of hand. Like last night when she'd found one of Finn's little blue socks wedged behind the couch cushion. She'd sank down with the soft scrap of cotton in her hand and boo-hooed like an idiot.

Well, she *wasn't* an idiot, and she *was* going to get past this. But she wasn't going to do it without some help. Bailey squeezed her eyes closed.

Dear God, help me get myself back on an even keel, because I honestly don't know how much more of this I can take. She waited, but she didn't sense any answer. *Please*, she added desperately.

Then she stiffened. Somebody was knocking on her front door. She swept a quick glance at the fitness tracker on her wrist and frowned. It was way too early for visitors. The only person she knew who'd be likely to show up at this crazy hour was...

Dan.

The broken handle still clenched in her fingers, Bailey jogged through the living room, finger-combing her hair with her free hand as she went. Breathlessly, she pulled open the door.

Abel stood on her porch, his lean face worried. Hoyt Bradley stood behind him, and he didn't look much happier than Abel did.

Bailey's hope tanked into disappointment, followed quickly by a little stab of fear. Abel wouldn't just show up like this without a good reason. "What are you guys doing out here so early? Has something happened to Dan?"

To her relief, Abel shook his head. "Far as I know, Dan's fine. I sent you an email saying that Hoyt and

I'd be coming out and to let us know if it wasn't convenient. Didn't you get it?"

"I'm behind on my email." She'd seen Abel's message in her inbox, but she hadn't opened it. She'd been feeling a little too raw for that. "Why'd you need to come by?"

"Well." Abel looked at Hoyt, who only shrugged uncomfortably. "Look, it's kind of chilly out here. Do you think we could talk about this inside?"

"Sorry. Sure." She stood aside to let them come in. As Hoyt edged past her, she noticed the large metal toolbox he was holding. She frowned as she shut the door behind them.

"All right, Abel. Spill it. What's going on?"

"I told you she wasn't going to like this," Hoyt muttered to Abel. "And I know I don't like getting in the middle of it."

Bailey's eyes narrowed. "In the middle of what?"

Abel held up a hand. "Now, don't get all ruffled up. It's simple enough. Before he left town, Dan hired Hoyt to finish up your repairs. He said what with the twins and having to head back to Wyoming quicker than he'd thought he would, he wasn't able to finish them. He didn't want to leave you in the lurch."

Dan had done *what*? Bailey fisted her hands on her hips as her emotions went into overdrive. She hadn't known a person could be so annoyed and so utterly touched at the same time. She turned her gaze to Hoyt, who set his toolbox down with a clank and held up his hands in surrender.

"Look, Bailey. None of this was my idea. Danny came asking me for a favor. We go way back, and I didn't like to say no, that's all."

"He didn't say anything to me about this. Not one word."

"You'd never have given him the go-ahead," Abel answered easily, his eyes skimming the house as he spoke. "Like they say, it's easier to ask forgiveness than to get permission sometimes. I don't see what the problem is, Bailey. You've got plenty to do around here if you want to get ready for that foster care inspection. And you already agreed to let Danny help you. He's just doing it long-distance, is all."

"Danny's put the money down for this job before he left town," Hoyt added. "So I hope you're not going to make a fuss. But the bottom line is, this is all up to you. I told Danny I couldn't work on your property without your permission."

Bailey listened silently, then looked at Abel. "Let me guess. That's why you came along, isn't it? Dan asked you to talk me into accepting the help. He figured I'd listen to you."

Abel shifted his weight from one boot to the other. "I reckon he thought maybe I could help you see the good in this plan of his, yeah. Look, Bailey, Danny just feels bad about leaving you in a fix, and he wanted to make sure these repairs got done as fast as possible."

"It's going to be weekends, though," Hoyt put in quickly. "Weekends and evenings. I'm snowed under at work. And just from what Danny told me and what I've seen so far, you've got a lot that needs doing. But I'll get it done—and done right."

"See?" Abel said encouragingly, "That's just what you need, isn't it? And I'll come out and help when I can, too. Don't let your pride get in the way of your common sense, Bailey. You've got a passel of work to do out here. You've got siding that needs replacing and a couple of windows, and from the sound of that dripping coming from your kitchen there, you've got plumbing problems to boot."

Bailey looked down at the faucet handle still clutched in her hand. "The kitchen sink blew up on me this morning. Sorry I can't offer you guys coffee, by the way."

Abel plucked the handle out of Bailey's fingers and tossed to Hoyt. "I reckon you'd best start by taking a look at that sink, Hoyt. And put a rush on it. Bailey without her morning coffee is nothing to play around with."

Hoyt disappeared into the kitchen. Abel shut the door behind the contractor and then turned back to Bailey, his face serious.

"You don't look so good," he said.

"I wasn't exactly expecting company at six thirty on a Saturday morning, Abel."

"That wasn't what I was getting at. Your eyes are all red, and you've got dark circles under them. You look like the raccoon I caught raiding the chicken coop last week. Only not as cheerful. What's wrong?"

"Nothing. Or at least nothing I can't get over."

Abel stood silently, his expression unreadable. "Danny told me he'd signed those divorce papers, and I was right sorry to hear it. I'd have been proud to keep you as my sister-in-law, Bailey."

Her heart constricted. "I appreciate that. But this was really the best choice, Abel. For me and for Dan."

Abel nodded slowly. "I reckon you're right. If you don't love him, then it's better you let him go."

The careful restraint in Abel's voice made Bailey

feel sick. She and Abel had been good friends for years, but this mess she'd gotten into with Dan was pulling Abel's loyal heart in two different directions.

She swallowed. "It wasn't that."

The lanky farmer's blue eyes sharpened. "Are you saying you do love my brother, Bailey? Because if you do—"

She cut him off. "It's more complicated than that."

"No, it's not, Bailey. If you two love each other, it's simple enough. It's just not easy."

"Abel, I don't want this to ruin our friendship, but you don't understand how things stand with Dan and me."

"I understand enough to know that it gutted my brother to leave you behind. I told him he needed to stop pushing you so hard, but when I saw the look in his eyes when he came to say his goodbyes to me and Emily... And now you're standing here looking like something the cat spit up." He shook his head. "I should have kept my big mouth shut."

"This isn't your fault, Abel."

"Maybe I should call Danny. If he knew how bad you're hurting, he'd—"

"Do what? Come back to me? He's not going to do that, Abel. And I wouldn't want him to. He made his choice."

"And you made yours."

"Yes, I have. And I won't apologize for it. I've thought long and hard about this, Abel. Staying in Pine Valley is the smart decision. I wish with all my heart Dan could have seen that, but he couldn't—or wouldn't. I can't help that, but I'm not going to ignore my own common sense to go along with him. Not this time." She was preaching to herself as much as to Abel.

Abel looked unconvinced. "For a person making such a smart decision, you don't look too happy about it."

"Maybe I'm not too happy, but I'm not sure that matters."

"Of course it does."

"Really? You know the happiest I've ever been in my life, Abel? I was eighteen, and I'd just kissed your brother in a county clerk's office in Tennessee, right after the man told us we were man and wife. We both know how that turned out. Sometimes the things that make us happy aren't the smart choice. Like chocolate, for instance. It might make me happy, but that doesn't mean it's good for me."

Abel sighed. "Maybe not. But then again, what's life without a little sweetness in it?" Her friend ran one hand through his shock of black hair. "You know, before he left, Danny said something to me about how he didn't have the right to ask you to trust him enough to chuck everything you've got here to follow him out to the ranch. But now I'm not so sure that you trusting Danny is really the problem here. Sounds to me like the real trouble is you don't trust yourself very much."

"Maybe there's a reason for that. I don't exactly have the best judgment where your brother is concerned. If I did, I wouldn't be feeling so bad right now because I know good and well that I can't afford to keep making the same mistakes. This isn't about losing my store, Abel, or this house. There's a lot more at stake than that. It's about losing *me*, the person I became after Dan left. I'm a lot smarter now. I'm a lot stronger. I've built a good life here in Pine Valley, a life that I'm proud of. I belong here. If I throw all that away just because your brother asks me to… Well, then I go right back to square one, don't I? I can't risk that."

Abel shook his head. "I admire you, Bailey. Always have. And you're right about one thing. You're one of the strongest people I know. Strong enough to bend a little for the people you love without breaking, I'm thinking. Of course you belong here, but a woman like you can make a place for herself anywhere she chooses to go. That's why I don't think you should stick with a life you've outgrown just because you're determined to play it safe."

Bailey made a wry face at her friend. "You're a fine one to lecture me about playing it safe, Abel Whitlock! You're still living a mile from the cabin you grew up in."

Abel didn't hesitate. "That's true enough. I never wandered far, but that doesn't mean I haven't taken more than my share of risks. I fell for my Emily the moment I laid eyes on her. You want to talk about losing yourself? It happened to me in a split second. I might as well have handed her my heart in a box with a bow on it, because it belonged to her just as sure as if I had. I had to wait years for her to feel the same way about me, but in God's good time, she did, and I married her. There are days when I still can't quite believe it really happened, when I wake up and think for a minute there it was all just a dream. There's nothing safe about loving somebody like that. You take it from me, Bailey Quinn. Falling in love is the riskiest adventure there is." He offered her a lopsided smile. "And the best."

Suddenly Bailey found herself blinking back tears.

"You're blessed to have found love so close to home, Abel."

Abel shook his head. "You've got it all inside out. I'd lived in Pine Valley all my life, but it was never truly my home, not until Emily came back with her two little ones in tow. Love's what makes this town my home, Bailey. Without it—" he shrugged "—this place is nothing to me but another dot on the map."

Suddenly a loud clatter came from the kitchen followed by a sound of gushing water. "Abel! Bailey! I need a hand in here. And a bucket! These pipes are old as dirt. The whole plumbing system's going to have to be replaced."

"Coming, Hoyt!" Abel ran toward the kitchen, but Bailey didn't budge.

She stood there quietly in the middle of the room, thinking hard about what Abel had said. Shouts, bangs and other frantic noises came from her kitchen, but she ignored them.

She was lost in a swirl of memories so vivid it seemed as if Dan was standing right in front of her.

Dan at nineteen, scarcely an hour after they'd gotten married, his face taut with hurt when she'd demanded he take her back home to her family. *"But I'm your husband now, Bailey. We're a family, just the two of us. Aren't we? That means our home can be anywhere we want it to be. Just as long as we're together."*

That very same pain had glimmered in his eyes when she'd argued with him about moving to Wyoming. *"I still want you to be my wife, Bailey. I want us to make a life together, be a family together, you and me and the twins. That's what really matters, isn't it? Where we live is just geography."*

Just geography.

And what was it that Abel had said? Something about love making a place a home.

She looked around the living room. This house had thrilled her the first time she'd walked through it. She'd seen all its flaws; of course she had. But none of that had mattered. The run-down farmhouse had caught at her heart because she'd felt confident that with a little work, she could turn it into a real home.

But it couldn't, she realized. No matter how hard she worked here, this place would never be a home. Not for her, not now.

Not without Dan and the twins.

Without the three people she loved best in the world, this endearingly ramshackle farmhouse, her trendy, successful little store…in fact, the whole of Pine Valley, Georgia, were nothing but…what was that expression Abel had used?

Nothing but dots on a map.

And somehow Dan Whitlock, the guy who'd grown up with the worst home situation she'd ever seen up close, had figured all that out before she had.

She'd been so worried about losing herself by reuniting with Dan and so determined not to surrender her hard won independence that she'd missed something big. She'd missed out on the fact that her feelings for Dan and the twins had become a huge part of who she was now—and of who she wanted to be. By letting them go to Wyoming without her, she'd lost not just them, but a lot of herself, as well.

That's why she was feeling so miserable and unsettled. Because most of her wasn't even here anymore. The heart she'd been so afraid to risk had simply packed up and moved to Wyoming without her.

Playing it safe had turned out to be the riskiest plan of all.

Oh, Lord, Bailey prayed sadly. *Please help me. I think I've made a really big mistake.*

Ten minutes later, a drenched Abel and Hoyt walked into her living room and told her sheepishly that they'd had to shut off all the water to the house and had no idea when it could be turned back on.

Bailey looked at the dripping men. "You know what? Leave it off." She reached for the hook on the wall and took down her key chain. "Hoyt, here's a key. Do whatever repairs need doing, okay?"

Hoyt took the key and nodded, looking relieved. "You got it. I'm going to start off by cleaning up the mess we just made in your kitchen. I'll be right back."

"Abel," Bailey said as soon as the contractor had squelched out onto her porch, "I need to buy a livestock trailer fast. Can you help me with that?"

"No need to buy one. I've got one you can use."

"I appreciate the offer, but I don't know when I'll be able to get it back to you." She met his eyes squarely. "Could be quite a while."

"I see." There was a short beat of silence as Abel studied her. "Going somewhere, are you?"

"You know what? I think maybe I am."

For a second, she thought she saw tears glimmering in the tall man's eyes, but he only shook his head and grinned. "Then you're welcome to the trailer and anything else I've got. After all—" he flung one wet arm over her shoulders, pulling her close and soaking her in the process "—you're family, Bailey Quinn. Or—"

He leaned closer and muttered in her ear, "Is it Bailey Whitlock now?"

"I'm not sure," she answered honestly. "But I'm ready to find out."

"Shh, buddy. It's okay!" In the ranch house nursery, Dan flexed his knees, bouncing a wailing Finn against his shoulder while he tried to change Josie's diaper one-handed. "Just let me get your sister fixed up, and we'll go downstairs and have breakfast."

Finn's fussing only got louder, and Dan winced. It was like the kid knew that once they all managed to get downstairs, there was still going to be some lag time as Dan heated up bottles and traded off feeding the twins.

Finn had an appetite like a horse, and he didn't like to wait for his food. And the problem was, the two little ones seemed to be connected. If Finn screamed, it always freaked out Josie, too.

"I can handle all things through Christ Who gives me strength," Dan muttered as he struggled to get the sticky tapes on Josie's disposable diaper in the appropriate spots. He hoped this one actually stayed on. He had about a fifty-fifty track record in that area lately, and there were a lot of tiny pink bloomers waiting in the laundry hamper.

He shot a quick glance at his scratched wristwatch. The vet was going to be here any minute to do those pregnancy checks, and Dan hadn't even started with the bottles yet. Finn was going to lose his mind.

What a day for the new sitter to cancel on him. Although he hadn't been all that surprised, really. The look on the older woman's face when he'd said "twins" had been a pretty clear warning.

He'd start a new babysitter search this afternoon, but for right now he'd just have to find a way to manage on his own.

"Come on, munchkins. Let's go downstairs and get some grub." He gently picked up both twins and started picking his way down the wide wooden stairs toward the kitchen. Sometimes movement calmed the twins down—Dan had spent half of last night pacing the floor with one twin or the other. But right now, nothing seemed to do the trick. Finn's crying had stirred Josie up, and both babies howled the whole way down the steps.

Dan's eye snagged on a photograph of Colt and Angie, and he sighed. He felt so strange living in the McAllisters' huge, echoing house. He knew it belonged to him now, at least until the twins were grown. He'd stowed away the McAllisters' personal belongings, rearranged the bedroom he'd picked out, trying to make it feel more like his own. It hadn't helped much. He still felt like a trespasser, like he'd overstepped his bounds somehow. If it wasn't for the babies, he'd have bunked out with the hands, but he'd figured the twins needed to be in their familiar nursery.

He'd hoped that once they were back on their home turf, the babies would settle down, but that hadn't happened. They were miserable, and so was he.

He was missing Bailey like crazy.

Even though he'd known that was coming, he hadn't been prepared for how the pain of leaving her had ramped up mile after mile. It had taken every bit of determination he'd had not to turn that truck around and head back to Georgia, take Bailey in his arms and promise her anything he could think of if she'd just throw out those stupid divorce papers.

But he'd driven on, bleary-eyed and exhausted, until he'd made it to the Bar M. The hope that his mood would improve once he was back on the ranch had flopped. If anything, he felt worse. It was like being away from Bailey was cutting off his air supply—he was slowly suffocating without her.

But the ranch needed him. He hadn't been back five minutes before he'd found out one of the prize bulls was limping, two of the ranch hands were in Broken Bow's county lockup, the tractor had a flat tire and the pregnancy checks were two weeks overdue.

It was a no-win situation, all right. The ranch needed him. And he needed Bailey.

He fumbled through the bottle routine in record time. At least he was getting a little better with the mechanical side of this childcare gig. Settling into a wide armchair, he tried his hand at feeding both twins at the same time. He had to steady Josie's bottle with his chin, but it worked, sort of. And that was a good thing, because just as he managed to get Josie to finish the last of her formula, he heard a truck pulling up outside.

The vet was here. Dan carefully laid Josie down next to Finn, who was already stretching and kicking on the quilt Dan had folded up on the floor.

On to the next problem—how to manage two babies while he briefed the vet about the bull and the pregnancy checks. In a situation like this, a man had to do whatever it took.

No matter how stupid it made him look.

Dan snatched up the pink flowered sling thing that

he'd found stashed in the nursery, still in its plastic wrapper. Going by the picture on the front, you fastened this around your middle and you could carry one baby swaddled up in it. If he could do that, then he could carry the other twin in his arms while he walked the vet out to the barn.

Unfortunately, fastening the thing wasn't as straightforward as he'd thought. Dan buckled the belt of the gizmo around his middle and started trying to sort out its folds. Meanwhile the twins scrunched up their faces and began to fuss.

"Just give me a minute here, guys. I've almost got this." He looped the thing over his arm. This couldn't be right. The baby-holding part was on his back now. Frustrated, Dan pulled his arm back out and snatched the crumpled directions back off the couch for another look.

A brisk knock sounded on the door. He'd better go answer it. Doc Andrews was the only vet in the county, and he was overworked and not particularly patient. If somebody didn't make it to the door fast enough, the vet would be backing up his truck in a split second, heading off to his next call.

"Hold on! I'm coming!" Dan shouted over the twins' fussy cries. He scooped them up and headed toward the door.

Then he stared at the doorknob, stymied. He had no free hand. "It's open!" he called finally. "Come on in!"

The door edged open. Dan found himself looking straight into Bailey Quinn's dark eyes, and the bottom fell right out of his heart.

In the back of his mind, he knew he should be saying something—probably a whole lot of very important stuff. But he couldn't manage a single word. All he could do was stare at her, like a starving man would stare at a buffet table.

She looked tired, but she had that determined, you-can't-tell-me-what-to-do look on her face. She tilted her head as the babies increased their wails.

"Well, you seem to have your hands full, don't you? Here. Gimme." She reached forward and scooped Finn out of his arms.

Her fingers barely brushed Dan's chest, but the touch felt like an electric shock. His brain stuttered back into action.

"What are you doing here?" Then he shook his head. "You know what? Don't answer that—not yet, anyway. Come in."

Bailey walked into the sprawling living room, and Dan used one boot to kick the door shut behind her.

She turned, and her eyes met his, searching them over the top of Finn's head. They were bouncing the squirming babies in perfect rhythm, which would have been funny if Dan hadn't known that everything that really mattered in his world was hanging on what happened in the next few minutes.

Dan tried to read Bailey's expression, but before he could make much headway, Bailey pulled her gaze away. She scanned the disheveled room, and when she looked back at him, she lifted an eyebrow. "It looks like a baby store exploded in here." She nodded at the frilly pink strap dangling off his shoulder. "And what's that about? Getting in touch with your feminine side?"

"I love you, Bailey." He hadn't meant to blurt that out, but he couldn't help it. "Before you tell me why you're here, I need to say my piece. I've been dying here without you. No," he added, as her eyes dipped to the twins. "This has nothing to do with the babies. Well, okay, yeah, they're helping kill me, but that's not what I'm talking about. I can figure out how to be a single dad if I need to. But I can't figure out how to live without you."

"Dan—"

He cut in. He had to say this. "I'll do whatever it takes to make this work for you, Bailey. I've never begged anybody for anything in my life, but I'm begging you right now." He reached out with his free hand and traced her cheek. Her eyes went misty at his touch, and a tear skimmed down and puddled above his thumb. He leaned close and kissed it away, whispering against her skin, "Stay with me, Bailey. Please. Marry me. Or I guess I should say—marry me all over again. Make a family with me. And I give you my word that I'll spend the rest of my life making sure you never regret it."

When Dan's lips brushed her cheek, a waterfall of feelings cascaded over Bailey, and she felt her knees trembling. "Dan," she began huskily, looking up into his eyes.

Before she could get any farther, the squirming baby in her arms went stiff and produced an impressively loud burp. Bailey and Dan locked eyes. All the crazy emotions clogging Bailey's throat got tangled up with her laugh and came out her nose in a snort.

Dan made a face at Finn, who was wide-eyed with surprise at the noise he'd just created. "Real romantic. You're not exactly helping me out here, buddy. Although—" Dan looked back at Bailey "—you might as well be clear on what you're getting yourself into, I guess."

"Danny Whitlock, you know perfectly well that I loved these babies from the first minute I laid eyes on them, so you can knock that off. Besides," she added, "Lucy Ball's outside in a trailer along with a bunch of really annoyed chickens. I think that evens up the score pretty well."

"What?" Dan leaned over and flicked a curtain aside to peer out the window. Sure enough Bailey's truck was attached to a livestock trailer, and he could see Lucy Ball's pink tongue flicking through, licking the rails. "You brought your animals with you?"

"Of course I did. I wasn't leaving them behind."

"But, then…you're staying?" The unabashed joy that broke over his face made her grin right back at him.

"That's the plan. If you'll have me."

"What about your store?"

"Well, I've been doing some thinking while you've been gone. I built that store from the ground up. What's to stop me from doing that again? People in Wyoming need to eat, too, don't they?"

"Yeah." A pained look crossed his face. "But then there's your house. You'll be giving that up, too."

"That doesn't matter. Turns out what I really want is a home, and no place feels like home to me without you. This one will suit me just fine." She glanced around at the expansive, wood-paneled room littered liberally with twin debris, and smiled. "It's got a lot of space. I like that—plenty of room for a nice, big family."

Dan shifted Josie in his arms and bent his head so

he could search Bailey's eyes. "You really mean that, Bailey?"

She met his questioning gaze squarely. "I do." She laughed softly. "That's the second time I've said those particular words to you, I believe."

"And this time's no more romantic than the first, is it? I'm sorry, Bailey. You deserve better."

She shook her head. "I sure didn't drive all the way out here for anything as flimsy as romance. I came here for love, a real love that won't fade out, and a real marriage with the man I can't live without. And that's you, in case you're wondering." She dropped a kiss on Finn's head. "Getting to mother these babies just sweetens the deal even more. Now do you think you could make this official and kiss me?"

"I do." He looked at her for a minute, his eyes gentle. Then he nodded slowly. "I surely do."

Dan leaned forward, angling so that Finn and Josie settled next to each other between them. And even though Bailey had already closed her eyes in anticipation of his kiss, she felt the warmth of his smile even before it met her own.

Epilogue

"Hold still." In the parking lot of the Broken Bow Community Center, Bailey Whitlock adjusted her husband's tie then stood back and tilted her head as she gave it a critical look. "Perfect. You clean up pretty well when you put your mind to it."

"I shouldn't be cleaning up at all. It's calving season. I should be in the barn. I don't see why they can't just mail me this plaque."

"For the twentieth time, because this is a big deal. You're the cattleman of the year. It's an honor." Bailey sneaked a look at her watch. It was nearly time for the ceremony to start. She scanned the parking lot. If her special guests didn't show up soon, she and Dan would have to go in without them. "Now behave. I didn't buy a new dress and put on these silly heels to listen to you fuss all night."

Dan's eyes flicked over her, and he smiled in that way that still made Bailey's heartbeat stutter, even though it had been over a year since they'd renewed their wedding vows. "If I didn't happen to mention it before now, you look beautiful, Bailey."

Bailey laughed. "I think you mentioned it twice before we got out of the driveway."

"Yeah, well. It's a long driveway." Dan leaned down
and kissed her. "You're always beautiful to me anyhow, heels or not, but they do put you in closer kiss-
ing range, so that's a plus. You sure you don't want to
forget about this and just go back home?"

"Nice try, but absolutely not. You're accepting this
award, and I'm going to stand up and clap like crazy.
If you're not proud of yourself for this, at least I'm
proud of you. Remember when people were posting
all that negative stuff about you online? And now look
at you. The ranch is already turning a tidy profit and
you're raking in awards. God's been good to us, and I
think we should take time out to celebrate. You'll get
back to work tomorrow, but tonight let's enjoy ourselves, okay?"

"I always enjoy myself when I'm with you. Okay,
we'll do this your way, but we're not staying out too
late."

A pickup turned into the parking lot, and Bailey's
heart jumped happily. They were here! "Don't start,
Dan. The guys can handle the cows for one night, and
Finn and Josie are perfectly happy with Carla. She's
their favorite babysitter, and she brought her stuff so
she could stay overnight. This is a special night."

And it was about to get a lot more special.

"I'm not worried about the twins or the cows, Bailey. But I am a little worried about you. You've been
looking tired lately. I think you're working too hard at
the new store. Ever since you landed that big spread in
the cooking magazine, you've been swamped. I know

you don't want to hear this, but I think you're going to need to hire more help."

"Okay. I'll set up some interviews next week."

Dan frowned suspiciously. "That was way too easy. What's going on, Bailey?"

"Excuse us. We're looking for the cattleman of the year. You got any idea where we might find him?"

Dan jerked around. "Abel!" He grabbed his brother in a fierce hug as Bailey embraced Emily.

"Thank you for coming," she whispered.

"Are you kidding?" Emily whispered back. "We're thrilled you invited us. We wouldn't have missed this for the world."

"I can't believe you came all this way just to see somebody hand me a piece of wood with my name on it," Dan was saying.

Abel coughed and shot Bailey a look. "Yeah, well. Bailey seemed to think it was important."

"It *is* important," Emily put in quickly. "They even did a story about it in the *Pine Valley Herald*. I have it posted up on the bulletin board in the coffee shop. How are Finn and Josie? I can't wait to see them!"

Dan kissed his sister-in-law on the cheek. "They're doing great. Maybe you can help me talk Bailey into cutting out of this thing early. Then we can make it back to the ranch before they go to sleep."

Bailey made a face. "Don't let him fool you. He has two Shadow Lady heifers about to deliver, and he just wants to get home to supervise."

"We passed your new store on the way in. It looks wonderful, Bailey, and your store back home is doing well, too. We all miss you, of course, but Johanna is doing a great job managing it. You'll see for yourself next time you guys come back to stay at the cabin. I can't believe you're a franchise now! Before long you'll have yourself a whole chain!"

"Don't give her any ideas. She's wearing herself out with just the two stores. Last night she fell asleep with her head on the kitchen table."

"Don't worry yourself, little brother. That's just the first trimester. Emily was the same. In a couple of months, Bailey will have more energy than she knows what to do with." Abel held open the door to the hall. "Is that steak I smell? Good. Last time I had to go to one of these award dinners, they served chicken. It tasted like plastic." Dan, Emily and Bailey all stood frozen on the steps. Abel looked at them. "What? What'd I say?" Then his eyes locked with Emily's, and his face fell. "Uh-oh."

"Bailey." Dan had to try three times, but he finally managed to get out his question. "Are you *pregnant*?"

"Abel, you ruined the surprise!" Emily turned stricken eyes to Bailey. "Oh, honey. I'm so sorry."

Bailey only laughed. Her eyes were fixed on Dan's face, watching his expression shift from astonishment to wonder.

And then to hope. He took a step toward her. "Is it true, Bailey?"

She nodded, and he swept her up into his arms. For a few seconds, the rest of the world disappeared.

When they finally drew away from each other, Abel cleared his throat uncomfortably. "I'm real sorry about that, Bailey."

She gave his arm a playful swat. "Don't be silly. Why do you think I told you in the first place? You've never kept a secret in your life. I knew you'd forget and say something sooner or later. Part of my fun was going to be waiting to see how you'd end up doing it. I have to say, though, I thought we'd at least make it out of the parking lot. Now come on, let's get inside. We can talk about all this after the ceremony."

"Careful, now," Dan worried aloud as they started up the steps. "Maybe those heels weren't such a great idea after all."

"Oh no, you don't, cowboy. I'm not about to let you wrap me up in cotton wool for the next seven months." Bailey sighed happily. "Having a baby is a perfectly natural thing, and I'm planning to enjoy every single minute of it."

"I can tell you from personal experience that every single minute of pregnancy isn't all that enjoyable," Emily said wryly from behind them. "But you hang on to that thought, Bailey."

"No," Dan said quietly. He tucked Bailey's arm in his and bent down to kiss her on the nose. "You hang on to me, sweetheart. You hang on tight."

Bailey laughed and gave his arm a squeeze as they walked into the banquet hall. "That," she said, "is exactly what I'm planning to do."

* * * * *

Dear Reader,

Hi! I want to thank you for taking this trip back to Pine Valley, Georgia, with me. How I have loved each visit to this sweet small town!

This particular story has been in the back of my mind ever since Bailey Quinn strolled into the barn in my first-ever Love Inspired novel *A Family for the Farmer*. I knew right away that a woman as feisty and full of personality as Bailey Quinn deserved her very own happily ever after! And who better to bring that to pass than Dan Whitlock, Abel Whitlock's prodigal brother—and Bailey's biggest secret? But of course, secrets and small towns just don't mix. And to make things even more complicated—while Bailey and Dan struggle to make sense of their crazy situation, Dan finds himself entrusted with a set of infant twins. What results is a story about faith and forgiveness, first loves and long-overdue second chances. I hope you enjoy it!

I'm always busy writing so hopefully we'll be taking another trip together soon! In the meantime, don't be a stranger! You can find me at my website, laurelblountbooks.com—and while you're there don't forget to sign up for my newsletter! I send one out every month, full of news, recipes and giveaways! You can also drop me an email at laurelblountwrites@gmail.com. I'd love to hear from you!

Warmest wishes,
Laurel Blount

WE HOPE YOU ENJOYED THIS BOOK!

Love Inspired®

New beginnings. Happy endings. Discover uplifting inspirational romance.

Look for six new Love Inspired books available every month, wherever books are sold!

AVAILABLE THIS MONTH FROM
Love Inspired

FINDING HER AMISH LOVE
Women of Lancaster County • by Rebecca Kertz
Seeking refuge from her abusive foster father at an Amish farm,
Emma Beiler can't tell anyone that she's former Amish whose family was
shunned. She's convinced they'd never let her stay. But as love blossoms
between her and bachelor Daniel Lapp, can it survive their differences—
and her secrets?

THE AMISH MARRIAGE BARGAIN
by Marie E. Bast
May Bender dreamed of marrying Thad Hochstedler—until he jilted her for
her sister with no explanation. Now, with Thad widowed and a single father,
the bishop insists they conveniently wed for the baby girl. When May learns
the real reason for his first marriage, can they rediscover their love?

A HOPEFUL HARVEST
Golden Grove • by Ruth Logan Herne
On the brink of losing her apple orchard after a storm, single mom
Libby Creighton can't handle the harvest alone. Reclusive Jax McClaren
might be just what her orchard—and her heart—needs. But he's hiding a
painful secret past...and love is something he's not quite sure he can risk.

HER SECRET ALASKAN FAMILY
Home to Owl Creek • by Belle Calhoune
When Sage Duncan discovers she was kidnapped as a baby, she heads to
a small Alaskan town to learn about her birth family—without disclosing her
identity. But as she falls for Sheriff Hank Crawford, revealing the truth could
tear them apart...

SNOWBOUND WITH THE COWBOY
Rocky Mountain Ranch • by Roxanne Rustand
Returning home to open a veterinary clinic, the last person Sara Branson
expects to find in town is Tate Langford—the man she once loved. Tate is
home temporarily, and his family and hers don't get along. So why can't
she stop wishing their reunion could turn permanent?

A RANCHER TO TRUST
by Laurel Blount
Rebel turned rancher Dan Whitlock is determined to prove he's a changed
man to the wife he abandoned as a teen...but Bailey Quinn is just as set
on finally ending their marriage. When tragedy lands Dan as the guardian
of little orphaned twins, can he give Bailey all the love—and family—she's
ever wanted?

Could this bad-boy newcomer spell trouble for an Amish spinster…or be the answer to her prayers?

Read on for a sneak preview of
An Unlikely Amish Match,
the next book in Vannetta Chapman's miniseries
Indiana Amish Brides.

The sun was low in the western sky by the time Micah Fisher hitched a ride to the edge of town. The driver let him out at a dirt road that led to several Amish farms. He'd never been to visit his grandparents in Indiana before. They always came to Maine. But he had no trouble finding their place.

As he drew close to the lane that led to the farmhouse, he noticed a young woman standing by the mailbox. A little girl was holding her hand and another was hopping up and down. They were all staring at him.

"Howdy," he said.

The woman only nodded, but the two girls whispered, "Hello."

"Can we help you?" the woman asked. "Are you…lost?"

"*Nein*. At least I don't think I am."

"You must be if you're here. This is the end of the road."

Micah pointed to the farm next door. "Abigail and John Fisher live there?"

"They do."

"Then I'm not lost." He snatched off his baseball cap, rubbed the top of his head and then yanked the cap back on.

Micah stepped forward and held out his hand. "I'm Micah—Micah Fisher. Pleased to meet you."

"You're not *Englisch*?"

"Of course I'm not."

"So you're Amish?" She stared pointedly at his clothing—tennis shoes, blue jeans, T-shirt and baseball cap. Pretty much what he wore every day.

"I'm as Plain and simple as they come."

"I somehow doubt that."

"Since we're going to be neighbors, I suppose I should know your name."

"Neighbors?"

"*Ja.* I've come to live with my *daddi* and *mammi*—at least for a few months. My parents think it will straighten me out." He peered down the lane. "I thought the bishop lived next door."

"He does."

"Oh. You're the bishop's *doschder*?"

"We all are," the little girl with freckles cried. "I'm Sharon and that's Shiloh and that is Susannah."

"Nice to meet you, Sharon and Shiloh and Susannah."

Sharon lost interest and squatted to pick up some of the rocks. Shiloh hid behind her *schweschder*'s skirt, and Susannah scowled at him.

"I knew the bishop lived next door, but no one told me he had such pretty *doschdern*."

Susannah's eyes widened even more, but it was Shiloh who said, "He just called you pretty."

"Actually I called you all pretty."

Shiloh ducked back behind Susannah.

Susannah narrowed her eyes as if she was squinting into the sun, only she wasn't. "Do you talk to every girl you meet that way?"

"Not all of them—no."

Don't miss
An Unlikely Amish Match *by Vannetta Chapman,*
available February 2020 wherever
Love Inspired® *books and ebooks are sold.*

LoveInspired.com

Get 4 FREE REWARDS!

We'll send you 2 FREE Books plus 2 FREE Mystery Gifts.

Love Inspired® books feature contemporary inspirational romances with Christian characters facing the challenges of life and love.

FREE Value Over **$20**

YES! Please send me 2 FREE Love Inspired® Romance novels and my 2 FREE mystery gifts (gifts are worth about $10 retail). After receiving them, if I don't wish to receive any more books, I can return the shipping statement marked "cancel." If I don't cancel, I will receive 6 brand-new novels every month and be billed just $5.24 for the regular-print edition or $5.99 each for the larger-print edition in the U.S., or $5.74 each for the regular-print edition or $6.24 each for the larger-print edition in Canada. That's a savings of at least 13% off the cover price. It's quite a bargain! Shipping and handling is just 50¢ per book in the U.S. and $1.25 per book in Canada.* I understand that accepting the 2 free books and gifts places me under no obligation to buy anything. I can always return a shipment and cancel at any time. The free books and gifts are mine to keep no matter what I decide.

Choose one: ☐ **Love Inspired® Romance Regular-Print** (105/305 IDN GNWC) ☐ **Love Inspired® Romance Larger-Print** (122/322 IDN GNWC)

Name (please print)

Address   Apt. #

City   State/Province   Zip/Postal Code

Mail to the **Reader Service:**
IN U.S.A.: P.O. Box 1341, Buffalo, NY 14240-8531
IN CANADA: P.O. Box 603, Fort Erie, Ontario L2A 5X3

Want to try 2 free books from another series? Call 1-800-873-8635 or visit www.ReaderService.com.

SPECIAL EXCERPT FROM

Love Inspired.
SUSPENSE

On the run from Witness Protection, Iris James can only depend on herself to stay alive…until a man she thought was dead shows up to bring her back.

Read on for a sneak preview of
Runaway Witness *by Maggie K. Black, available in February 2020 from Love Inspired Suspense.*

Iris James's hands shook as she piled dirty dishes high on her tray. Something about the bearded man in the corner booth was unsettlingly familiar. He'd been nursing his coffee way longer than anyone had any business loitering around a highway diner in the middle of nowhere. But it wasn't until she noticed the telltale lump of a gun hidden underneath his jacket that she realized he might be there to kill her.

She put the tray of dirty dishes down and slid her hand deep into the pocket of her waitress's uniform, feeling for the small handgun tucked behind her order pad.

Iris stepped behind an empty table and watched the man out of the corner of her eye. He seemed to avert his gaze when she glanced in his direction.

A shiver ran down her spine. As if sensing her eyes on him, the bearded man glanced up, and for a fraction of a second she caught sight of a pair of piercing blue eyes.

Mack?

Mack's body had been found floating in Lake Ontario eight weeks ago with two bullets in his back. This man was at least ten pounds lighter than Mack, with a nose that was much wider and a chin a lot squarer.

She glanced back at the bearded man in the booth.

He was gone.

She pushed through the back door and scanned her surroundings. Not a person in sight.

She ran for the tree line and then through the snow-covered woods until she reached the abandoned gas station where she'd parked her big black truck.

Almost there. All she had to do was make it across the parking lot, get to her camper, leap inside and hit the road.

The bearded man stepped out from behind the gas station.

She stopped short, yanked the small handgun from her pocket and pointed it at him with both hands. "Whoever you are, get down! Now!"

Don't miss
Runaway Witness *by Maggie K. Black,*
available February 2020 wherever
Love Inspired® Suspense books and ebooks are sold.

LoveInspired.com